NURSE WITH WINGS

Everyone at Wirrumburra Hospital welcomed Karen, except the man who counted most, the Medical Director, Guy "King" Kendall. Yet despite the sparks they struck from each other, despite their fiery disagreements, they seemed to be drawing more closely together. But could this mean anything, Karen wondered, when Guy Kendall was so obviously set to marry the beautiful and determined blonde Terri Lawson.

NURSE WITH WINGS

Nurse with Wings

by
Judith Worthy

MAGNA PRINT BOOKS
Long Preston, North Yorkshire,
England.

British Library Cataloguing in Publication Data.

Worthy, Judith
  Nurse with wings.
  I. Title
  823(F)   PR9619.3.W6/

  ISBN 0-86009-966-0
  ISBN 0-86009-967-9 Pbk

First Published in Great Britain by Mills & Boon Ltd, 1979

Photoset in Great Britain by
Dermar Phototypesetting Co, Long Preston, North Yorkshire.

Printed and bound in Great Britain by
Redwood Burn Limited, Trowbridge, Wiltshire.

CHAPTER ONE

His hands were cool and impersonal, the spread fingers of one scarcely touching the warm skin of her bare back, the other loosely clasping her fingers as they danced in a rather sedate old-fashioned way.

He might have been wearing surgical gloves for all the sensation this contact engendered, and what was more—with a shock Karen realised it—suddenly, she was no longer vulnerable. The revulsion that even the thought of another man's touch had always aroused was gone. She just felt numb now, as though her skin no longer had any nerve ends. There was no flood of passionate memories to quell, but there was nothing else either. She didn't expect there to be—ever. No man, she knew, would ever arouse her emotions by a mere brush of his fingertips the way Sean had done. Nevertheless, there was relief in being able to think of him for the first time without a rending of her heart.

'Do you go there often?' her partner asked

quietly, with a faint smile.

Karen's eyes flicked up to his face, puzzled. 'Go where?' Wasn't the joke to say 'Do you *come here* often?'

The smile became quizzical and his light hazel eyes regarded her with concern.

'Wherever it was, you were there for two whole circuits of the dance floor. By your expression it wasn't a particularly happy place.'

Karen took a deep breath and let her gaze slide across his suntanned features capped by a shock of thick light-brown hair. He was nice, this latest blind date that Linda had dug up for her, quite the nicest in fact that she had ever let herself be bullied into going out with.

Miles Curtis was his name, Dr. Miles Curtis. She was being a boor, Karen knew, not talking much, scarcely smiling, barely even polite, but experience had taught her to remain aloof. It avoided having them all over her like a rash at the end of the evening and usually discouraged a follow-up phone-call asking for another date. Whatever they said to Linda about her afterwards, Linda never revealed, but her expression often spoke volumes. Karen always felt guilty and wished she had not let Linda organise her, yet she never seemed able to muster the strength to counter Linda's persuasiveness, and Linda, bless her really, was the kind of girl who never gave up on a friend.

More contrite than usual, Karen said apologetically, 'Sorry, I was drifting there for a bit.' She searched her mind for details about him that Linda might have relayed to her and found nothing much, or perhaps she simply had not been listening when Linda had prattled on about him. She did, however, recall one thing.

'You're down from the north, aren't you?'

He nodded. 'I'm at Wirrumburra Hospital.'

'On holiday at the moment?'

'More or less.'

He was not a chatterer. Or a flatterer, Karen thought, which was probably why she liked him and felt more comfortable with him than she had with anyone else she had met during the past months. He had not said one word about her softly clinging green silk halter-neck dress, or that the colour matched her eyes exactly. He had not remarked on her bright burnished-copper hair that fell in soft waves to her smoothly tanned shoulders, but Karen was not disappointed even to realise that in all probability he had scarcely noticed.

His hazel eyes regarded her with interest, even some speculation, but showed no special

11

interest in her physical attributes.

She wondered, as always, what Linda had told him about her. Linda knew very well that she did not want pity, so it was unlikely she would have told him about Sean's tragic death after a long illness—over a year ago now—and how she had given up nursing because she could not bear the sight of sick—and especially dying—people; and she would not have told him either that he was the umpteenth blind date that she had foisted on Karen in an effort to bring her back into the real world, as she put it.

Karen often wondered why she just didn't flaty refuse to go to the balls, parties, dances, barbecues and other social functions which Linda constantly dragged her along to, but the inertia that had made her unable to resist at the beginning was now a habit. Besides, deep down she knew that she had wanted to go because of a masochistic need to be hurt over and over by the sharp scalpel-thrust memories of Sean that accompanied each outing. Except tonight ...

Karen half smiled to herself. Perhaps Linda had been right and time would eventually heal the wound. On the surface at any rate. Tonight, being with Miles Curtis did not hurt. Tonight, for the first time, she did not feel the ghostly arms of Sean holding her close, his lips brushing her hair whenever she closed her eyes. She felt absolutely nothing. It made her curiously light-headed, as though she'd inhaled too much ether—but she wasn't nursing now ...

Miles was saying something but the music at that moment rose to a crescendo and she missed it. The chords died away as the dance ended and Miles was guiding her back to their table. The others in the party were also drifting back with laughter and talk and Karen caught Linda's eye, sharply questioning and gleaming with the faint hope that her friend might at last be enjoying herself again.

Dear Linda, Karen thought with a sudden rush of affection. Who else would have bothered with her for so long and so faithfully? Karen felt guilty. What a misery she had been all these months, what a drag! The irritation she had sometimes felt at Linda's persistence had vanished and she felt immense gratitude instead. She smiled at her friend and immediately Linda's face lit up although she said nothing.

'Are you nursing at the same hospital as Linda?' Miles was asking and dimly Karen was aware that he had asked the question before and she had not answered.

'No. I gave up nursing nearly a year ago,' she said, trying to keep the tremor out of her voice. 'I'm a secretary now.'

He looked surprised but he did not ask why she had given up nursing, as everyone else did, so for once there was no need to make excuses. Karen dreaded explanations and was relieved she did not have to make any now.

After a moment, however, he said, 'Don't you ever want to go back to it?'

She was a little startled by the unexpected question. 'To nursing? No, I don't think so.' Curiously, she felt unsure for the first time. Nursing had been her whole life—until Sean.

He regarded her intently. 'Oh, I rather got the impression from Linda ... well, as a matter of fact we need an extra two nurses at Wirrumburra and I'm looking for candidates. I don't suppose you'd ...'

'No!' It came out rudely because she was angry with Linda for presuming to suggest she might want to return to nursing. Instantly she was ashamed, because her feelings were changing, she now realised, but it was too soon yet, much too soon. 'I'm sorry,' she murmured. 'No, I really don't want to go back to it. Thank you for asking me, but I'm quite happy doing what I'm doing at the moment.'

'Are you?' he asked quietly, and the way his

kindly eyes regarded her made her feel she had betrayed herself in some way.

They danced and he did not bring up the subject of nursing again. He did not mention hospitals or medicine at all. He did not ask her to talk about herself and he did not talk much about himself either. Karen enjoyed the impersonal flavour of the evening, the lively discussion on subjects of general interest, and felt more at ease with Miles than she had in a man's company for a long long time.

Even Linda was more restrained than usual. She did not ask eagerly, in the powder room, how Karen was getting along with Miles. She merely remarked that Karen's dress was very becoming and that the suntan she had acquired during the first week of her holiday suited her.

Miles drove Karen home after the dance. She thanked him and said goodnight.

He detained her with a light touch on the arm. 'Perhaps, if you're not doing anything tomorrow ...?' he asked hopefully. 'I've borrowed this car for my stay and we could ...'

'I'm sorry,' she cut in quickly, though for once feeling churlish about it. 'I'll be busy tomorrow.' He looked so disappointed at the rebuff that she felt she had to explain. 'I always go flying on Sundays.'

'Flying?' He looked startled.

She laughed. 'My wings are the aluminium kind!'

His face showed surprise and interest. 'Well, I'll be ... you never mentioned it and Linda didn't say ...' He trailed off in amazement.

There was every reason why Karen should not have mentioned it to him. She had avoided personal subjects all evening and the last thing she would have wanted to discuss was flying. That was her private world, the world she had shared with Sean, and up there in the limitless blue sky she could sometimes imagine that her shadow on a cloud was Sean's plane alongside her, that she was close to him.

She said offhandedly, 'Should I have?'

'No, except that ...' A smile crossed his lips but he did not finish the sentence. He said instead, 'I don't suppose I could persuade you to take me for a spin?'

Now she felt trapped. A good excuse for refusing just would not come into her head and she could not explain why she preferred to fly solo.

So she said flippantly: 'You're game, aren't you?'

'Why? You've got a licence, I hope!'

'Of course, but some men don't seem very keen to fly with a woman pilot.'

He laughed. 'Heavens, I'm not one of them!'

He looked down at her intently. 'Karen, I'd really love to come.'

She could not understand his insistence and neither could she see a convincing way out of the dilemma, or perhaps, she reflected later, it was simply that she did not really want one. The prospect of spending Sunday with Miles Curtis, she discovered as she removed her make-up later and brushed her hair, was, astonishingly, a rather pleasant one.

As arranged, Miles called for Karen next morning. She was almost ready, dressed in a blue denim skirt and jacket with a pert denim cap covering her hair which she had pushed up under it. She was just pulling on her boots when the doorbell rang.

Miles looked casual and carefree in cream slacks and safari jacket, and younger, Karen thought, than he had last night. There was something very boyish and appealing about him as he smiled and said good morning. Miles was just the sort of brother she would have liked, she decided in some amusement.

'You're still game then?' she asked teasingly, picking up her shoulder-bag.

'Naturally!'

There was something about him this morning that Karen could not quite fathom. He was cheerful and casual and yet underlying his carefree manner was hesitancy, as though he had something important on his mind, and she had the oddest feeling that it concerned her because he kept glancing at her in a thoughtful and speculative way.

Less than an hour later, at the airfied from which Karen's flying club operated, she was taxi-ing the tiny single-engined aircraft she always flew along the runway. She glanced at Miles and he grinned at her and nodded reassuringly. Karen waited briefly for her clearance to take off and then they were speeding down the concrete.

As always she was filled with a tremendous sense of exhilaration as the aircraft lifted off the ground and soared into the air. There was always for her just a slight tension as she climbed the vital first few hundred feet, but the moment she levelled out it vanished and the peace that being in the air brought settled over her.

There was a feeling that flying gave her that was impossible to describe adequately. It was too personal and could never be accurately transmitted to another through words. For Karen flying was something she had always wanted to do—like nursing. Meeting Sean, who was an instructor for a local flying school, had been a kind of miracle, especially when she had fallen in love with him and he with her.

By skimping and saving she had managed to afford to take lessons and had finally passed all the tests and examinations and gained her licence. Sean had owned his own plane and so because of his generosity she had been able to clock up many more hours flying time that she could otherwise have afforded. He flew home on many weekends to his parents' country property and whenever she was off duty she would go with him, usually taking over the controls for one way at least. Now she flew in memory of Sean and felt closer to him up there in the sky which had meant so much to him. Always when she flew her thoughts were exclusively of Sean.

But not today. Today she could not think of Sean except in a strange detached kind of way. She was too conscious of her passenger. He seemed relaxed enough, as though accustomed to flying in light aircraft, but he did not talk much. Talking always seemed irrelevant anyway to Karen, except when necessary, and she was delighted that Miles felt the same.

They stayed up for over an hour. It was a bright clear day with a few puffs of white cloud above and very little haze on the ground. The view was fantastic and Karen for some strange reason felt more relaxed than she had for a very long time.

They followed the coastline at first and then circled back over the suburbs and city until finally Karen brought the plane in to a perfect landing and taxied up to the hangar where she handed it over to the engineers.

Later, as they were leaving the airfield, Miles said, 'Lunch?'

'Thank you,' Karen answered, 'but you really don't have to ...' He had not said a word yet, she realised, about how he had enjoyed the flight. Perhaps he hadn't after all. She felt a bit disappointed, as though it must be her fault, so she was reluctant to prolong the occasion.

He was however not to be put off. 'We passed a likely looking place on the way here,' he suggested. 'About a kilometre or so back along the highway. Is it okay?'

'You mean the Westerner? Yes, the food is good there. We often used to ...'

She stopped abruptly. She and Sean had often stopped for a meal there and she had not been since. She did not want to go now but she could hardly say so.

'That would be very nice,' she murmured.

They were seated at a table and had ordered

when Miles finally said, 'I enjoyed the flip, Karen. You're a very competent pilot. How long have you been flying?'

She felt ridiculously pleased at the compliment. 'Oh, a few years now.'

'Ever thought of making a career of it?'

She laughed. 'I don't see myself piloting a Jumbo Jet somehow!'

His face was deadly serious. 'No, but what about combining flying with nursing?'

Involuntarily she flinched. 'But I ...'

He leaned across the table and said earnestly, 'We could do with you at Wirrumburra. We've got a doctor-pilot now but he's a New Zealander and he's itching to get back home. Last time he was over there on holiday he met a girl and got engaged, but his fiancée doesn't want to leave her family to live in Australia. You could take his place and solve one of our nurse problems at the same time.'

Karen was stunned. This was the last thing she had expected Miles to say and it was the last thing she had ever considered doing, although now that he had put the idea into words it seemed crazy she had never thought of it herself. Two years ago perhaps she might have, but not now.

She said, 'But I thought the Royal Flying Doctor Service ...?'

Miles was nodding. 'We liaise closely with them, of course, but,' he laughed softly, 'in Kendall's Kingdom, things work a little differently.'

'Kendall's Kingdom?' The phrase rang a distant bell somewhere in her mind but she was still puzzled.

'Guy Kendall,' said Miles. 'You surely must have heard of him.'

Slowly a recollection surfaced mistily in Karen's mind. 'Yes ... yes, I remember now. There was a documentary on television about him, about a year or so ago?'

Miles nodded again. 'Guy didn't care much for the publicity. He prefers to keep a low profile and just get on with the job. You remember what it was all about?'

'Not very well.' It had been around the time of the complications in Sean's illness, she felt sure, and she had not been taking things in properly at that time. She had sat alone night after night in her flat watching television, too worried to concentrate on anything properly.

'It was the television reporter who dubbed the area Kendall's Kingdom,' Miles told her now, 'and it caught on locally. Not a bad description really, when you consider that Guy owns a pretty sizeable chunk of the country around Wirrumburra.'

'But I thought he was a doctor, not a station-owner.'

'He's both. He inherited a couple of sheep stations a few years back from his father and uncle. Both have managers but Guy, being Guy, keeps his finger on every pulse.'

'I still don't see ...' began Karen doubtfully.

The waiter brought their main course and while they ate, Miles told Karen about Kendall's Kingdom.

'When mining came to the north, a lot of things changed, as you must be aware. Wirrumburra changed. Guy was in the thick of it. To cut a long story short, he organises all medical services for the town and surrounding area, which includes stations and aboriginal camps and outlying mining camps. There's still a lot of exploration for iron and oil going on up there and quite a few people scattered around. Guy's father owned a private plane, so Guy now uses it to run his own aerial medical service. He doesn't fly himself neither do I, so that's why I'm looking out for someone to replace Alex. I was expecting to have to settle for just a pilot, since medics who fly are fairly thin on the ground.' He laughed suddenly. 'I must admit I never thought of a nurse with wings! But why not?' He gazed at her earnestly. 'Won't you consider it, Karen?'

She was still too taken aback at the idea to answer at once. In spite of herself she was interested and intrigued. Nursing and flying ... Kendall's Kingdom ... it was a temptation. But she had vowed never to nurse again.

'I've given up nursing,' she said in a flat tone. 'I haven't nursed for a year.'

Suddenly he reached across the table and clasped her fingers tightly.

'Karen, you can't hide forever. There must come a time when ...'

'No!' She withdrew her hand angrily. She knew Linda must have told him about Sean after all. She turned her head away. 'Linda had no right ...'

'Karen, don't be angry with Linda. I knew there was something desperately wrong with you last night, so I phoned her this morning before I came to pick you up. I more or less forced the truth out of her. Karen, look at me!'

Slowly Karen turned her head back and stared glassily at him. He took hold of her hand again and this time she did not draw it away.

'Karen,' he said in a low sympathetic voice, 'you're only half a person while you turn your back on what you most want to do. You're not truly happy away from it, are you? Be honest with yourself.'

'But I can't ... I couldn't bear ... I can't talk

about it, Miles. Please don't make me!' She simply could not bring herself to tell Miles the real reasons she had given up nursing, how her sense of failure, the feeling that somehow Sean's death was her fault, had taken root so that she could not assist at an operation without her hands shaking, her eyes misting over, and how in the end she had been afraid she would do something dreadful. It went too deep to explain.

Miles said quietly, 'You don't have to talk about it. I understand. But you can't waste your life, Karen, just typing letters and taking phone calls.'

'That's useful, too,' she protested.

'Sure, but not when you've been trained to do something else, something you really want to do. You know your fears are groundless, Karen, don't you? And you know you weren't to blame. You know everything possible was done—it always is.'

She stared at him. He knew without her telling him. He had seen right into her heart and recognised her anguish. She took a deep breath. 'I know. It's not logical but ... well, emotions aren't, are they?'

He smiled gently. 'Come back, Karen. Combine both your very special talents and start afresh. You can't live on memories forever, and you've so much to give.'

'Now you make me sound selfish,' she murmured, chastened.

'We are all selfish when our feelings are hurt, especially in grief, but sooner or later we have to think of others again. You became a nurse in the first place because you wanted to help others, didn't you?'

Mutely she nodded.

'Well, then?'

She met his gaze head on and his light hazel eyes had a challenging glint. There was a terrible tug-of-war going on inside her, a longing to say yes and yet a very real fear that she could not succeed. She stirred her coffee and did not answer him.

Finally, after they had finished, Miles said, 'Think about it, Karen. I'll be going back in a week's time. You can contact me through Linda.' He added casually, 'By the way, Linda's taking the other nursing post and I think I've found a doctor to take Alex's place. You'd fit into the picture perfectly—if you'll come.'

Karen was astonished to learn that Linda was going to Wirrumburra. 'But Linda's a city girl through and through, she'll hate it!' she exclaimed.

Miles laughed. 'I dare say, but she's adventurous and she says she wants to take a look at the outback. I'm not taking any bets on how long she'll last but,' he grinned shyly, 'maybe if her friend goes along, too ...'

Karen's mouth twisted in a faint smile. 'And how long do you suppose I'd last?'

He levelled a steady look at her. 'I think you have lasting qualities,' Miles said.

CHAPTER TWO

A week later Karen, the new doctor and Miles flew to Wirrumburra. Karen had had no difficulty in giving up her secretarial job. Her boss was an understanding man who had recognised that, efficient secretary though she was, her heart was still in nursing even though she was reluctant to admit it. He told her it was too exciting an opportunity to turn down and urged her to take it.

In a whirl of last-minute preparations Karen vacated her flat and packed her suitcases and could hardly believe how her life had changed in the course of a week. Linda did not fly with them as she could not leave the hospital at such short notice. She was to follow in a fortnight's time.

It was Karen's first taste of this part of the outback. She had lived on a farm with her parents as a child, but they had long since given up the property and retired to a seaside suburb of the city. They had been glad she was taking the job at Wirrumburra even though it meant they would see less of her. When she broke the news to them Karen suddenly realised, as relief flooded her mother's face, just how anxious they had been about her, how upset they were because she had given up nursing, and what a miserable time they, too, had been having this past year, because they worried about her.

As she was leaving she kissed them and said jokingly, 'Don't cheer yet, I might be back in a week!'

Her father had clasped her two hands tightly inside his. 'Not you, Karen. You've got more guts than that.'

Karen fervently hoped she had as she looked out of the plane window at the dry red country below, relieved only by occasional clumps of dull grey-green gum trees, pock-marked by hummocks of spinifex, scarred by the twisted scribblings of dry creek beds, and the horizon flat and unbroken except where a range of stark red hills glowed like burning coals in the late afternoon sun. Karen felt misgivings for Linda, too, and more than a little guilty.

She was certain that her friend had agreed to accept a post at Wirrumburra because she believed that Karen would be more likely to be persuaded if she did. When Karen taxed her with this and assured her that she did not have to do it for her sake because she had made up her mind to go, Linda had laughed and said she would not dream of breaking her promise to Miles now, anyway.

'Besides, I really think I might enjoy the experience,' she had said, adding mischievously, 'I think Miles is rather dishy even if you don't!'

Karen, nevertheless, had the strong conviction that Linda intended to be on the spot so that she could not chicken out too soon, even after starting the job.

Karen was sitting beside Miles, her thoughts far away, so that when he suddenly spoke in her ear, she jumped.

'Almost there, Karen.' He pointed out of the window and through the haze Karen saw a loose sprawl of iron roofs reflecting the sun. So that was Wirrumburra. From the air the neat orderly rows of buildings lay spilled between two low ranges of red-brown hills looking for all the world like some abandoned and forgotten toy town.

The aircraft began to lose height. Karen eventually lost sight of the township as they came in to land. A few moments later they had taxied to a halt in front of a long low wooden building with a shimmering corrugated-iron roof. Beyond was another large iron building shimmering in the heat, a hanger, One or two light aircraft were standing nearby.

'That's *Jabiru*,' said Miles, pointing. 'Ours.'

'A stork!' Karen exclaimed, laughing.

'Well, a baby or two has been born on board!' said Miles. 'Think you can handle her?'

Karen contemplated the gleaming silver plane a little apprehensively.

'I expect so. I haven't actually flown that type before, but I don't suppose I'll have too many problems. I don't know about babies as well, though!'

Miles laughed. He said, 'Alex will take you on a couple of familiarisation flights, for sure.'

This was confirmed a few moments later when they were met by Alex Cable, who was to drive them into Wirrumburra. He looked a little surprised to find that his replacement was a woman, but he welcomed Karen with a warm handshake.

'I'm sure glad to see you,' he said, with a cheerful grin.

'When are you going back home?' Karen asked.

The sandy-haired New Zealander grinned again. 'Now that you're here, just as soon as Guy gives me the nod.' He looked sheepish. 'It's been ages since I saw Eileen.'

31

Miles joked, 'She's probably run off with another fellow by now, Alex.'

'She'd better not!' They both laughed.

Dr. Lou Frinton, a tall dark-haired man in his thirties who had a slow smile and did not talk much, shifted his lanky form. 'Let's get to some shade,' he said. 'I'm boiling alive.'

Karen screwed up her eyes and pulled her sunglasses down from the top of her head where she had propped them during the last minutes of the flight. Miles led the way to the car park carrying one of Karen's suitcases as well as his own. He cast a sidelong glance at her.

'Well, glad you came? '

Karen tucked a strand of hair under the headscarf she had wound around her hair. 'Of course,' she replied with a smile and saw his frown relax. Miles was obviously still worried that she might change her mind even at this stage. She moved closer and said firmly, touching his arm, 'Don't worry, Miles, when I make up my mind to something I stick to it.'

His expression was rueful. 'Sorry, I didn't mean to doubt you. I'm sure you do.'

Miles opened the boot of Alex's car and he and Lou Frinton methodically stowed the luggage. On the way into town Karen sat in the back with Miles while Lou Frinton sat in front with Alex.

It was a long narrow dusty road into town from the airfield and the vistas on either side were hardly inviting, that is what you could see through the clouds of red dust. When they reached town, however, the road improved noticeably and Karen saw to her relief that the town was neither as small or desolate and abandoned-looking as it had seemed from the air. It was not large, either, but it evidently had a good water supply because the houses they passed all had neat colourful gardens with green lawns. Sprinklers sprayed the lawns, giving the streets a cooler aspect than the temperature suggested. When Karen remarked on it, Miles said:

'It was Guy who got the artesion water for the town. He hammered the authorities and the mining companies and even put his own money behind it. Guy really made things move here when he came back.'

'Came back?' Karen asked. She had thought of the legendary figure of Dr. Kendall as always having been there.

'After he finished his training he did a stint in Sydney and London,' explained Alex over his shoulder. 'I believe he came back about five or six years ago. Before our time.'

'From what I've heard he's pretty exacting to

work for,' commented Lou Frinton rather drily, but not as though the knowledge bothered him at all.

Karen had a feeling that nothing would rattle Dr. Frinton, at least he would not let anyone see that it did. At first when they had been introduced she had thought him rather cool and aloof, but when he smiled there was a warmth in his eyes belying his dry taciturn manner.

Miles said, 'Nobody runs rings around Guy, if that's what you mean. He has very high standards but doesn't expect anyone to do more than he does himself. I'd say he's fair, wouldn't you, Alex, if a bit stubborn sometimes?'

Alex nodded as they drove through the gateway of the hospital. 'Single-minded would be more my description,' he said generously. 'But work always comes first, the hospital, the people, the town, before everything else.'

Lou Frinton groaned. 'He sounds like a bit of a fanatic.'

Miles laughed. 'I must admit it sometimes seems like it, but you've got to hand it to him, Guy Kendall makes things happen, at least he does around here.'

'He sounds formidable,' remarked Karen, as they drew up outside the main hospital building. A small quiver of nervousness fluttered her heart. What if she could not live up to this man's high standards? She had been a whole year away from nursing and she did not know how she would react when first faced with assisting at an operation. Deep down there was still a fear that she would at worst go to pieces, at best tremble like a leaf, or perhaps just freeze and then run ...

Miles was opening the door for her. 'I'll take you both in and introduce you,' he said, 'and then we'll go round to Ma Carson's place. That's where you'll be staying, Karen.'

Alex said, 'I'll drop your bags off there for you, Karen.'

Karen murmured her thanks and, slinging her bag over her shoulder, tucked her sunglasses in the top pocket of her crisp white cotton shirt and smoothed down her dark blue linen skirt. She tried to swallow the little lump of nervousness jumping up and down at the back of her throat, and wished she knew how to look as cool and unconcerned as Lou Frinton did.

She glanced briefly at the hospital, a long, low, white-painted weatherboard building shaded by gum trees and flaming poincianas. Perspiration began to trickle down the back of her knees and she swiftly dabbed her forehead with a handkerchief as they walked

35

towards the entrance, again feeling envious of Dr. Frinton who looked so cool and collected in his fawn safari suit.

To her relief they were greeted by cool air as they entered and she heard the whirr of air-conditioning. Miles paused at the reception desk and spoke to a nurse who was sorting record cards.

'Hello, Kelly, missed me?'

The girl grinned. 'Hi, Miles. Yeah, like a dose of malaria! Have a good trip?' Her gaze shifted briefly to Karen and Lou. 'I heard you'd been successful.'

'This is Sister Karen Lalor,' said Miles, drawing Karen closer. 'And Dr. Lou Frinton. Nurse Kelly Maguire.' He grinned sidelong at Lou. 'Watch her, Lou, she's dynamite. Ask the fellows up at the mine!'

The nurse nodded and murmured a friendly 'hello' and then slapped Miles' chest playfully. '*You* watch it, Dr. Curtis! Or I'll get the biggest to take you on!'

Miles laughed and said, 'Guy around?'

'He was in theatre a while ago,' Nurse Maguire said. 'I don't know if he's through yet. It was old Davey Potts, Miles. They found him on the backsteps of the pub this morning. Fractured patella this time, I gather.'

'Poor old Davey,' said Miles. He turned to

36

Karen. 'Local personality. Always falling over and breaking something.' He exchanged a meaningful smile with Kelly. 'There's a good reason for the instability, which I expect you can guess. Guy always keeps him in longer than necessary if we've got a spare bed so he can dry him out a bit, so I suppose he does himself a good turn breaking a bone or two now and then. He's an old prospector, a real old-timer, over eighty if he's a day. He'll jaw your ear off if you let him.'

'And pinch your bottom!' said Kelly with a laugh. She looked Karen over. 'Well, I hope you're going to like it here. As soon as you've settled in I'll organise a get-together with some of the girls. Okay?'

Karen felt a surge of warmth that was nothing to do with the weather. It was the easy-going informality of this place, the friendliness and casual manner of her first encounter that lifted her spirits. The hospital did not seem at all the kind of austere place she had imagined that such a man as she had expected Guy Kendall to be would rule. Perhaps he was not so formidable after all. She had a sudden strong feeling that she was going to like working here very much.

'Let's go along to Guy's office,' said Miles, leading the way through a door off the reception area. 'If he's not there, we'll see Matron first and by then he'll probably be through.'

Dr. Guy Kendall was not in his office and Karen knew a fleeting feeling of disappointment. She was anxious to meet the man and see for herself just what he was like, to get the interview over with and oddly enough, to start work. Suddenly she itched to put on a uniform again, to slide her feet into spotless white shoes ...

Miles continued on down the corridor and knocked on Matron's door. A deep strong voice bade them enter.

'Miles, you're back! Guy's operating, did you know?'

A tall athletic-looking woman in her mid-fifties, Matron Muriel Fawkes rose from her desk and strode to meet them.

'Yes, so I thought I'd introduce Karen and Lou to you first,' said Miles.

If her uniform was starchily stiff, Matron herself was not. She shook them both warmly by the hand and bade them all sit down. Karen warmed to her immediately, and even Dr. Frinton seemed to be smiling more openly as they chatted. After five minutes or so the door suddenly opened without any preliminary knock.

'Ah, Guy.' Matron's voice cut across what

Miles had been saying, and Karen and Lou Frinton both turned curiously to look at the man who had entered the room.

Karen was instantly aware of a commanding presence. A very tall figure stood right behind her chair, overshadowing her and as she looked up she met the searing gaze of dark gunmetal-grey eyes beneath black brows and crisp dark hair.

'How's old Davey?' Matron asked.

Dr. Kendall shrugged. 'He'll be laid up for a spell, but that won't do him any harm.'

As he spoke the telephone on Matron's desk rang and as she answered it, Dr. Kendall remarked, 'You might as well all come along to my office, Miles.'

He turned abruptly and went out. Miles rose, signalling Karen and Lou with a glance, to follow him. In his office Dr. Kendall sat down and motioned them to do likewise. As Miles introduced her, Karen found herself subjected to prolonged and flinty-eyed scrutiny. Although his penetrating gaze made her feel very uneasy she instinctively felt one other thing—that Guy Kendall was above all an excellent doctor. It was strange, but she could always sense ability the moment she met a new doctor. She could recall instances in the past where the feeling had been strong, others

39

where it had not, and invariably her intuition had proved right, and in the latter case the doctor eventually proved to be adequate but not outstanding. Dr. Kendall was quite clearly outstanding. What he was like as a person she was unable to tell at all.

He said to Miles, 'Well, I'm glad you were so successful, Miles. It was a relief to get your telegram.' He smiled briefly at Karen and Lou and went on crisply, 'No doubt Miles has explained to you already how things are organised here, so I won't waste any of our time on procedures. I'm sure you'll both slip into our routine very quickly. The atmosphere here might be a little different to what you're accustomed to but I don't think you'll find any trouble getting used to it, and I hope you'll both settle in without any problems. If you do have any, I am here to solve them.'

Karen and Lou both nodded and murmured thanks. It was clear that Dr. Kendall did not intend to prolong the interview.

He said, 'Have you any questions you wish to ask now?'

Both shook their heads. Miles had already provided detailed briefing so there was nothing either wanted to know at present.

'Very well then,' concluded Dr. Kendall, rising, 'I'm sure you're both anxious to settle into your accommodation and have some rest.'

Miles glanced at Karen and smiled. 'Clinic day tomorrow, Karen. We leave early. Take-off's at eight, so you'll need to be at the airfield before that, but Alex will give you the low-down on all that when ...'

'Just a minute, Miles,' Dr. Kendall's interruption was sharply surprised. 'There's no need for Sister Lalor to go on the clinic circuit tomorrow. Nurse Morwell is rostered.'

Miles looked a little taken aback. 'But, Guy, even so it'll be good practice for her to make a trip with Alex. Some of those airstrips can be a bit of a problem.'

Dr. Kendall glanced at Karen, slightly puzzled and obviously annoyed because his directive was being queried. 'I really don't see what the condition of the airstrips has to do with Sister Lalor,' he observed a shade sarcastically. 'She will be fastening her seat belt, I trust, in case of a bumpy ride.'

Miles said a trifle impatiently, 'I just thought she ought to do the circuit with Alex before she has to do it by herself. I'm sure she's keen to, aren't you, Karen?'

'Well, yes, naturally,' Karen said, a little warily. 'It could only help to get some idea of the terrain at first hand with someone else at the controls, particularly as I haven't flown

41

your type of aircraft before.' She smiled hopefully, wondering why Dr. Kendall seemed so opposed to her having a practice run. She would have thought it was the kind of thing he would insist on, with his reputation for thoroughness.

She was unprepared for the expression of angry astonishment that transformed his face as she finished speaking. He stared at her as though she had suddenly turned green or something equally horrifying and then wheeled on Miles.

'Miles, your telegram said ...' He picked up a piece of paper from his desk and waved it briefly, then read from it in a measured voice, '..."Arriving Monday with pilot nurse and doctor stop second nurse following in fort-night".' He glared at Miles accusingly.

'That's right,' agreed Miles. 'The pilot-nurse is Karen, Sister Lalor, and ...' He glanced at the telegram Dr. Kendall shoved at him. 'Oh, Lord, I see now ... they didn't put the dash between pilot and nurse!' He laughed sudden-ly. 'Good grief! No wonder you got the wrong idea. Sorry, Guy, I didn't realise you'd mis-understood. I thought you realised that Sister Lalor is our pilot, too.'

There was a momentary hush. All eyes turned to Karen and she felt her cheeks turning scarlet for no reason at all but that. It was a moment of silence that seemed like an eternity and all because of the expression on Dr. Kendall's face. He looked as though he was about to explode.

He spoke eventually in a tightly controlled voice. 'I'm sorry, Sister Lalor,' he said. 'I didn't realise the true position or I would never have let you come all this way for nothing.'

Karen was stunned, unable at first to take in his meaning. 'For ... nothing?' she stammered stupidly.

'I'm afraid the job is not for a woman,' explained Dr. Kendall bluntly, his eyes raking Karen's slight, rather fragile-looking figure with a gleam of contempt, but a man's look nonetheless. He shifted his gaze to Miles. 'I would have thought you would have realised that, Miles.'

Miles looked as taken aback as Karen and then embarrassed. 'Guy, I don't see what difference ...' he began but was abruptly cut off.

'It makes all the difference in the world,' insisted Dr. Kendall emphatically. 'I'm sorry, Sister Lalor, but it's just not on.'

His arrogant dismissal of her capabilities just because she was a woman incensed Karen. She felt her anger rising rapidly. She had coped before with men who didn't think women could or even should fly, but usually they capitulated in the end and admitted that women were as good as men, sometimes better.

'I've been flying for several years, Dr. Kendall,' she informed him coolly, drawing herself up stiffly and speaking in a haughty voice that belied her nervousness. 'I am as competent as any man, I assure you. Dr. Curtis has flown with me and he can tell you ...' Her voice rose angrily as she tossed her coppery head.

A peremptory wave of his hand stopped her flow. 'Competence isn't enough for this job,' Dr. Kendall said flatly. 'It requires a cool, calm temperament, stamina and the ability to think quickly in emergencies. Without wishing to offend you, I'm afraid I consider a man a more suitable candidate for the job.' His eyes rested briefly on her flaming red hair as though he was considering that a pointer to her temperament, and again snaked down over her slim but shapely body. The sensuousness of his glance doubly irritated her.

'I'm also a nurse,' Karen retorted hotly, 'and nurses are taught to be cool, calm and collected in a crisis, and I would imagine you are well aware, Dr. Kendall, that nursing requires a good deal of stamina. I was nursing for six years before I ...' She stopped abruptly and her chin jutted challengingly as she looked him full in the face, but his gaze was unrelenting.

'Before you what?' he queried curtly.

She was trapped. He would have to know, of course, but now was not a good moment to explain.

'I ... I've been a secretary for the past year,' Karen muttered lamely.

'Oh, you gave up nursing? Why did you do that?'

She could not tell the truth. He was clearly not the kind of man to understand. 'I ... I just wanted a change for a while,' she said lamely.

Miles put in, 'Karen has excellent references from her last hospital.'

Dr. Kendall's mouth quirked ironically. 'I should hope so,' he remarked.

Karen seethed but managed to remain silent.

Dr. Frinton then spoke in his quiet way. 'They have women pilots nowadays in the Royal Flying Doctor Service.'

He received a cold stare from Dr. Kendall for his pains. Karen shot him a brief smile of thanks and before Dr. Kendall could speak again she burst out, 'I think it's unfair to pass judgement on me when you haven't even seen how I can do the job. I'll fly your plane tomorrow if you like and you can take Dr. Cable along as well just in case I botch it!'

Her eyes flashed and sparkled angrily but

it made no difference to him.

'Yes, Guy, why not at least give her a chance now she's here,' said Miles, trying a cajoling tone but clearly very put out by the unexpected turn of events. 'If Alex gives her the okay ...'

'I give the okays here.' Having bluntly silenced Miles, Dr. Kendall gave Karen a slow condescending smile. 'I really don't think there's any need to wrangle over it, Sister. This is a tough job with long distances to travel and many unexpected hazards like flooded airstrips, dust storms, cockeyed bobs, and I long ago decided that it was not a suitable job for a woman. That is final.'

Although she was close to tears of frustration and disappointment, Karen fired back hotly, 'That's quite ridiculous! Absolutely illogical! A man is just as likely to ditch you in a dust storm as I would be!'

He observed her cynically. 'Have you had any experience of dust storms, Sister Lalor, or flooded airstrips, or being sucked into a cockeyed bob?'

'No, but ...'

'That is my point,' he said triumphantly. 'I'm afraid that tripping around metropolitan airfields and touring the suburbs on joyrides is not sufficient qualification to tackle this job.'

'I've been on many long country trips,' she

46

tried desperately, 'and I know how to handle an aircraft in all kinds of conditions. Just because I haven't yet met some of them ... I don't suppose you wouldn't tackle an unfamiliar operation, Doctor, in an emergency. You'd expect your general competence to carry you through, I'm sure.' She saw a slight smile lift Dr. Frinton's mouth, but Miles looked appalled at her daring.

'We are not discussing my competence!' snapped Dr. Kendall.

'No! A man's competence is always taken for granted, isn't it?' she threw at him recklessly. 'Well, let me tell you there are plenty of men who will fly with a woman without getting the jitters or feeling upstaged! I used to fly my fiancé and he never worried about me ditching him in a thunderstorm, or a cockeyed bob!'

The steely eyes still did not waver but one eyebrow twitched. He had evidently not expected her to be so argumentative. Dr. Kendall said caustically, 'Even if I were to agree to your staying there would be little point as you have just admitted you are engaged. No doubt you will want to get married in the not too distant future and leave. I'm afraid I need someone more permanent than that.'

Since Alex Cable was leaving to be married,

47

and he was a man, the point seemed irrelevant, but Karen was tired of arguing with this implacable man. She decided to set him right on one point, however.

'My fiancé is dead,' she said, evenly, 'and I have no intention of getting married, not for a very long time, if ever.'

For a brief moment there was a flicker of something in his eyes that might have been sympathy but he did not make the customary remarks that people usually did.

He merely said, 'Perhaps that is how you feel now, but from what I have seen so far and from what you have told me, you appear to have a rather volatile and impulsive nature. How do I know you won't suddenly rush off, if not to get married, to become a secretary again or a bus conductress or whatever takes your fancy for a while?' She was silent as he regarded her ironically. Then he went on, 'I can understand your disappointment, Sister, at being brought up here on a wild-goose chase, but it is quite pointless arguing about it. If you wish to stay on as a nurse of course you may do so, but if not then Dr. Curtis will arrange for your return to Perth. If you do not wish to make your decisions at once, you can let me know tomorrow what you wish to do.'

His patronising tone and his overbearing

manner incensed Karen still further, but she could see that she would never win a battle with Dr. Kendall as her adversary. Nothing was going to budge this man from his fixation. It was, however, a matter of pride that she should give him her decision at once. 'Thank you for the option, Dr. Kendall,' she said, 'but I'm sure I can find somewhere else to use my talents as a nurse *and* a pilot. I should like to return to Perth as soon as possible, please.' How could she stay and work alongside him, she thought, after this? It would be impossible.

'Very well,' he said, and again his eyes slid over her in a long narrowed look that made her shiver. There was something magnetic about this man in spite of his icy manner, his arrogance and his implacability. It could be a very rewarding experience to work with Dr. Guy Kendall, she thought, just so long as you did not hate him, of course, and at that moment Karen hated Dr. Kendall more than any man she had ever known.

CHAPTER THREE

As Miles slid into the driving seat of the car beside Karen, only moments after the dreadful interview with Dr. Kendall, he said, 'I'm sorry, Karen, I didn't think for a minute he wouldn't ...' He was lost for words.

They were alone, as Dr. Frinton was waiting for Alex Cable to return and take him home to the flat which the new doctor would in due course be taking over.

Tears of anger and frustration blurred Karen's eyes. She realised that above all else she was bitterly disappointed. She had been excited about this new and challenging job. The prospect of it had made nerving herself to return to nursing that much easier. It was so galling to have all her hopes dashed by the boorish and pig-headed Dr. Kendall. But clearly there was no possibility of changing his mind. Dr. Kendall ruled the roost around here and had made it perfectly plain that he would not be shaken in his decisions.

'No, I don't suppose you did,' Karen murmured with a wry glance at Miles. 'You're a reasonable man!' She pulled her hair back with both hands distractedly. 'Oh, what an arrogant, narrow-minded ...' She stopped, lost for suitable epithets.

Miles started the engine. 'Well, I'd better take you along to Ma Carson's anyway.' He glanced at her sympathetically and said hopefully, 'I don't suppose you'll change your mind and stay just to nurse?'

She shook her head, looking at him desperately. 'Oh, Miles, how could I? I couldn't face him day after day.'

'It'll be a blow to Linda,' Miles said, turning sharply out of the driveway on to the road. 'I wonder what she'll do now.'

Karen had temporarily forgotten Linda. Now she clutched her forehead. 'Oh, heavens, I hadn't thought of her in all the fracas. Miles, I'm sure she wouldn't have thought of coming but for me.' She glanced at him anxiously. 'Maybe she'll want to change her mind ... oh, Miles, that means you'll be back to square one, no pilot, no nurses.'

Miles' mouth was a grim line. 'Alex is going to be disappointed, too. He's desperate to get away as soon as he can. He'll be furious with Guy.'

'But even if I stayed it wouldn't help him,'

51

said Karen. She added, 'Maybe he'll be so mad he'll just walk out.'

Miles shook his head. 'I doubt it. He's on a contract. It's got another six months to run, like mine. Guy was willing to release him if we got a replacement, but he won't otherwise. If Alex shoots through he'll lose his end-of-term bonus, and as that's quite substantial and as he's getting married I doubt he'll want to forfeit it. Guy was going to pay him anyway even if he left before time. Besides, Alex isn't the sort to leave anyone in the lurch. He wouldn't let Guy down.' He turned into a side street and drew up with a squeal of brakes outside a house. 'Damn Guy!' he exclaimed feelingly.

Ma Carson was a weathered stick of a woman in her sixties with smoke-grey hair and piercing blue eyes. At first Karen thought her sharp wrinkled features and distant manner off-putting, but she soon changed her mind. Ma Carson showed her to her room which she would later share with Linda and told her to come along to the sitting room for a cup of tea. Karen soon discovered that Ma Carson had been looking after nurses from the hospital for almost as long as the hospital had been there and that under her somewhat austere exterior there was a kind and understanding woman with a real sense of humour.

'I do think it's most unfair,' she was saying as Karen came into the sitting room. 'Not even to give the lass a go.' She sighed. 'Still, I suppose he has his reasons and he thinks they're valid. This is tough country ... hello, dear ...' She broke off and smiled at Karen, immediately continuing, 'And I have to say, dear, that you're so slight and pretty that you hardly give the impression of being able to cope with it.'

'Size is no indication of strength and beauty doesn't give a clue to intelligence,' said Miles.

'Of course, I agree,' said Ma Carson, and laughed. 'Look at me! When my husband died they said I'd never run the station single-handed but I did, for many years.'

'Maybe you could persuade Guy to change his mind about Karen,' suggested Miles, smiling.

She shook her head. 'No, I don't think I could. He knows what he wants and he does what he thinks best. If he's sometimes wrong, well, no one is infallible.'

Karen detected a strong regard for Dr. Guy Kendall in her tone so she refrained from saying any more about him except a resigned, 'Well, it'll have been an experience, I suppose, just to come up here for a couple of days.'

Presently Miles left, promising to return in

an hour to take Karen to dinner at the local club. Karen showered and changed into a cotton dress and brushed her hair vigorously. The heat and shower had made it rather limp but she managed to coax some bounce back into it.

Dinner with Miles was scarcely a cheerful affair. Miles was very morose, clearly put out because he had assumed Guy Kendall would accept Karen as pilot-nurse without question, and also feeling responsible for Karen's disappointment. Karen was at pains to reassure him that she did not blame him in the least and that now she had taken the plunge she would still return to nursing elsewhere, even if without the involvement of flying, too.

'I guess it was just a bit too good to be true,' she said ruefully.

Alex Cable joined them later for a few minutes and Miles broke the news to him. When she saw Alex's bouncy cheerful face fall, Karen felt really sorry for him. His disappointment was as great as hers, if not greater, and illogically she felt as though she was the one who had let him down.

He left them saying, 'I think I'll go and get drunk!'

'Not too drunk,' cautioned Miles. 'Clinic day tomorrow, don't forget.'

'Who cares?' said Alex more flippantly than

he meant, Karen was sure. 'Serve him right if he has to make other arrangements.'

'And what would serve whom right?' The voice was smooth as honey with scarcely a trace of nasality. Its owner dropped a slim suntanned hand on Alex's shoulder. Karen looked up and saw a stunningly attractive woman with softly curling blonde hair framing large doe eyes and a wide mobile mouth. If there was a hint of hardness in the brown eyes, a little too much sharpness in her nose and the slight down tilt of her lips, this did not detract from her beauty.

'Hi, Terri,' said Miles with, Karen thought, a faint note of resignation as though he did not particularly like the girl.

'Hi, Terri,' echoed Alex and covered the slim hand with his in a light pat. 'I was talking about your boyfriend, sweetie. King Kendall.'

Her eyebrows rose and she withdrew her hand from his shoulder, stiffening slightly at the sarcastic tone. 'Why, what's Guy done?'

'Nothing much. He's just being bloody-minded about Karen,' Alex said bluntly, 'which means I'm stuck here after all.'

'Indeed?' Terri sat down and smiled vaguely at Karen, a smile that showed most of her even white teeth but barely acnknowledged Karen's existence and held no friendliness. 'You're Karen, I presume?'

'Sorry,' said Miles. 'Karen Lalor, Terri Lawson.' He stretched out his hands, palms uppermost, one in each girl's direction, as he introduced them. The two nodded and murmured appropriately, each wary of the other.

'And what,' Terri inquired archly, 'is Guy being bloody-minded about, may I ask?' Her eyes held Alex's defensively.

'Look, Terri, it's nothing to get het up about,' interrupted Miles placatingly, obviously not anxious to discuss the situation with the girl.

'Alex seems to be,' she commented drily. Then she shrugged. 'Oh, well, I dare say he'll tell me his side of it if it's all that important.' Her words suggested a close intimacy with Dr. Kendall.

Miles sighed. 'It's simply that I hired Karen as a pilot-nurse to replace Alex, and Guy won't wear it.'

Terri broke into laughter. 'Oh dear!' She looked Karen over and murmured obliquely, 'Well, I can't say I'm surprised.' Karen was not sure whether this opinion referred to her or to Dr. Kendall.

'Hey,' put in Alex enthusiastically, 'maybe you could persuade him, Terri. He might listen to you. Get him to give Karen a chance, that's all she wants. You can probably twist his arm better than anyone. Make him see how unreasonable he's being. It's hardly fair to drag the poor girl all the way up here and then send her back on the next plane without even a trial. Poor old Miles feels responsible, and last but not least, there's me. I was banking on getting away at the end of the week. I sent Eileen a cable as soon as Miles' telegram came and now I've got to send another cancelling all our plans. She'll be ...' He broke off and looked appealingly at the blonde girl.

Terri had turned her gaze to Karen as Alex was speaking and it was apparent straight away that she had no intention of interceding on Karen's behalf. To Karen's astonishment she plainly saw instant dislike in the other girl's eyes, though why Terri Lawson should dislike her on such brief acquaintance she could not guess.

Terri turned back to Alex. 'Well, of course I'd like to help, Alex, but frankly I don't see that it would be any use my trying to change Guy's mind. You know him. Once he makes a decision that's it. Still,' she finished airily, 'I'll see what I can do.'

'Thanks,' said Alex and Miles together but Karen knew instinctively that Terri had no intention of even trying.

'By the way, have you seen him?' Terri now asked, standing up again and looking round the crowded bar. 'I thought he might be here, that's why I dropped in.'

'Maybe he's held up at the hospital,' suggested Miles.

'No, I tried there,' she said. 'Oh, well, perhaps he'll be home by now. I'll call in again.' She swirled off saying, 'See you!' in an offhand manner.

'Do you think she'll have any luck?' asked Alex anxiously.

'What, in changing Guy's mind?' said Miles. 'I doubt it. She won't want to antagonise Guy by sticking up for Karen, I'm afraid.'

'No, I guess not,' said Alex gloomily. He stood up, 'Well, see you later. Enjoy your brief stay in Wirrumburra, Karen. I'll run you to the airfield when you're going. Miles will check the time of the next flight south for you.'

After he had gone, Miles said, 'I'm sorry it's turned out this way, Karen. Still, you might end up being grateful, I suppose. Wirrumburra is just about the end of the earth.'

'I wouldn't have minded that,' said Karen thoughtfully. 'I rather like the wide open spaces and it seems a pleasant little town. I'm not really a city girl like Linda, you know. I grew up on a farm.'

She felt sad again at the thought of having to give up this new adventure before it had even begun. And chagrined. As Miles had said earlier, 'Damn Dr. Kendall!' she thought.

Miles said, 'I suppose you could always take your case to the Equal Opportunities Board.'

Karen shook her head. 'No! Imagine his fury if I won.'

Miles nodded resignedly. 'But you won't stay as a nurse?'

Karen considered the prospect yet again. She hated the idea of letting Linda down but she just couldn't imagine working here alongside Dr. Kendall in the circumstances. She shook her head. 'No, Miles, I don't think I could. It's better to go now. I hope Linda will understand.'

Later Miles drove her home to Ma Carson's and at the front door he again apologised for the mess-up.

'Miles, I wish you'd stop apologising,' Karen said, slightly irritated now. 'It really doesn't matter. There's no need for you to be so upset about it.'

'I am upset,' he said emphatically. 'I feel I got you up here on false pretences. And Linda, too.'

There was nothing else Karen could say. She

said goodnight and went inside.

Karen was awake early next morning. She had spent a restless night and when she did manage to snatch some sleep her rest was troubled by dreams in which Dr. Kendall loomed threateningly over her ordering her to go. Since she could hear faint sounds coming from the direction of the kitchen, which must mean that Ma Carson was already up and about, she decided to get up herself.

She was just emerging from the bathroom when she heard voices and one of them was Miles'. She was about to go into her room when she heard him say, 'I'm sure Karen won't mind, and it is important.'

Karen, curious, tied her robe around her tightly and ran barefoot along the passage. Miles was standing just inside the sitting room with Mrs. Carson and they both looked startled to see her. Miles, she thought, had a gleam of triumph in his eyes, quite different to last night's downcast look. Her heart leapt. Was it possible Dr. Kendall had relented after all? She hardly dared to hope.

'Karen, you're up!' Miles looked pleased. 'I was just trying to persuade Ma to wake you.'

'I'd just had my shower,' Karen said, 'when I heard your voice. I wondered what had

brought you here so early in the morning.'
Suddenly she was aware of Ma Carson's disapproving gaze and realised what a picture she presented with her damp clinging hair and skimpy bathrobe and bare feet.

At that moment a kettle whistled and Ma Carson hurried out, with a slightly admonitory glance at Karen.

'Well?' queried Karen impatiently. 'What is it, Miles? Why are you here so early? I didn't think there was a plane today.'

He was smiling broadly now. 'Something's come up.'

'He's changed his mind?' Karen watched Miles' face carefully as she spoke.

Miles said, 'It's clinic day today, as you know, Karen.'

'Yes?'

'Alex kept his promise last night,' Miles told her drily. 'He got drunk. He doesn't drink much as a rule, so it didn't take much to give him one hell of a hangover this morning. He's not fit enough to fly a kite, let alone an aircraft. He's got a head like a sofa with the stuffing out, he says, so Karen, here's your chance!'

Karen sank on to the arm of a chair. 'You don't mean that Dr. Kendall has actually agreed to let me ...' She trailed off incredulously.

'Can you be ready in half an hour?' Miles asked briskly, glancing at his watch, and not answering her question directly.

'Well, yes ...' Karen answered hesitantly, feeling somehow that something was not quite right, and yet Miles wouldn't be here asking her to hurry if Dr. Kendall had not changed his mind.

'What did he say?' she asked.

'Look, never mind the details now,' said Miles. 'Do you think you can fly the *Jabiru* without instruction from Alex? I can tell you everything else you need to know, and Guy knows the country like the back of his hand anyway.'

Karen took a deep breath and let it out slowly. Then she tossed her head determinedly and gritted her teeth. 'I guess so,' she said, with more confidence than she actually felt.

Miles clapped her reassuringly on the shoulder. 'Good on you, Karen. Now get a wriggle on and then you'll have time for a good run over the controls with one of the engineers if necessary.'

Karen ran back down the passage to her bedroom and quickly threw on a pair of brown slacks and a white T-shirt. She wound a brown scarf around her hastily swept-up hair and tucked the ends under, grabbed her shoulder-bag and sunglasses and sped back to Miles who was pacing the sitting room sipping a cup of tea.

Ma Carson entered as Karen arrived and urged her to have breakfast, but Karen did not want to waste any time. She rushed out with a piece of toast in her hand to placate her landlady's anxieties and she was glad she had taken it, as munching it helped to quiet the butterflies in her stomach as Miles headed for the airfield.

When Miles finally skidded to a halt in the car park, Karen noticed for the first time that it was not his own car they were in. She glanced at him questioningly.

'This is Alex's car, isn't it?'

He grinned. 'Yes.' He reached into the back seat and dragged out a khaki battle jacket and a peaked cap, dumping them in her lap. 'Put 'em on!' he ordered.

'Miles, why?' She was instinctively alarmed.

'Flight gear. Alex always wears this rig when he's flying,' Miles informed her.

The penny dropped. Karen was shattered as she realised what Miles intended her to do. 'No!' she exclaimed, pushing aside the items of clothing as though they were red hot. 'No, Miles, you can't expect me to disguise myself as Alex! You're crazy!'

He laughed and got out of the car. He opened her door, and she tumbled out and faced him indignantly. 'Miles, this is ridiculous!'

'Look, Karen,' he said seriously, grasping her shoulders as though he feared she might cut and run. 'You want to prove you can do the job, don't you? Well, this is your only chance. Do yourself, Linda and Alex ... and me ... a favour. Give it a go. Prove to Guy that I made a good choice.' He shook her slightly. 'If Guy realises that it's you before take-off he might just turn stubborn ...'

'He'll be furious! He'll probably order me to turn back anyway.'

Miles shrugged. 'I doubt that. I know Guy pretty well. He won't fool about. Doing the circuit will come first.'

'I don't like it, Miles,' protested Karen doubtfully.

His grip on her shoulders tightened. 'Karen, don't let us down. Alex is depending on you.'

Karen eyed him suspiciously. 'I suppose he's not as hungover as you pretended. You cooked this up between you?' She wriggled out of Miles' grasp. He held out Alex's cap and jacket to her challengingly. She did not like the idea of deceiving Dr. Kendall. It would be different

64

if he had agreed to fly with her, but he hadn't. And he still might not. She bit her lip. Leaping up to crush her doubts was the strong desire to prove to Dr. Kendall that she was competent. She took the cap and jacket reluctantly from Miles.

'As soon as he slams the door,' said Miles as she struggled into Alex's gear, pulling the cap down hard on her head and tucking the scarf up under it as far as she could, 'start moving. He'll be in a hurry and he likes a quick getaway.' He laughed but Karen could only raise a faint smile.

'I still think it's utterly mad,' she said, but nevertheless walked swiftly besides Miles to the hangar in front of which stood the *Jabiru*. The engineer tinkering with it glanced at her approvingly and grinned. Evidently he was not surprised to see her in Alex's gear. He was in the plot, too. Miles must have been up very early this morning, she reflected, or else very late last night.

Miles quickly gave Karen a run-down on what the circuit entailed, showing her a map of the area and then said, 'Guy will guide you, don't worry.'

Karen was worried. Now she was not so much worried about the confrontation with Dr. Kendall as flying the unfamiliar aircraft.

Her mouth felt dry as the dust on the runway. She climbed aboard and settled herself behind the controls. Automatically she went through her checks, familiarised herself with the unfamiliar and found to her relief that there was not after all very much to worry her there.

Miles called to her, 'I'm off now. He'll be here in a minute. I want to keep out of sight until you've gone. Good luck!'

Shakily she nodded and waved to him, unable to speak. The engineer grinned up at her and gave the thumbs up sign.

'She flies like a bird,' he called. 'No worries, Karen!'

Something about the confident ring of his voice chased all her fears away and restored her own confidence. Also her stubborn determination. She would show Dr. Kendall, that she could fly his aircraft as well as any man.

A few moments later, parked opposite the administration building, she saw the cloud of dust. Guy Kendall was arriving along the airfield approach road. She knew a moment of real panic and then laughter bubbled up inside her. Whatever the outcome of this crazy enterprise she would be able to laugh about it later. She was quite mad, she knew, even to hope that Dr. Kendall would change his mind, but one's hopes are always highest, she

66

thought wryly, when the cause is the most hopeless.

The cloud of dust subsided and seconds later a tall athletic figure in short-sleeved shirt and trousers strode with long impatient strides across to the parked aircraft. Karen immediately averted her head and as the door swung open she contrived to be fiddling with something on the floor so that only her battle-jacket-clad shoulders were visible.

'Morning, Alex,' came the brisk, efficient voice of Dr. Kendall and there was a thump as he dumped his medical kit in the cabin. Karen did not answer and trusted he would think it was because she was too engrossed in what she was doing.

Guy said, 'We're on our own today, Alex. Nurse Morwell is sick, for heaven's sake, and Matron can't spare anyone else. I don't know what's the matter with her, either. She kept me hanging about for some footling query, most unlike her and on clinic day ...' Karen heard him moving about behind her, then the door slammed shut and he was still talking as he scrambled into the seat beside her as the aircraft began to move forward. She was not paying too much attention to his words now but she heard him mutter, 'It's a pity Miles had to go and bungle things, Alex ...' and then he stopped.

The break told Karen that the farce was over and her deception discovered. She steeled herself for the tirade to come and at the same time kept her mind on the controls of the unfamiliar aircraft.

Eventually he spoke again, loud and clear and with his fury barely controlled.

'Sister Lalor!' he barked so close to her ear that she felt the warm rush of his breath. 'This is not in the least clever or funny. I see now that there has been quite a conspiracy to put you in the pilot's seat this morning, but I suggest you end this foolishness immediately.'

The conspiracy, Karen suspected, had extended to Nurse Morwell and Matron, and she could not help but feel immensely grateful to them, because they would no doubt incur a good deal of his wrath when he returned.

She gritted her teeth and did not do as he commanded but turned on to the runway ready to take off.

'If you're going to do the circuit today,' she said as calmly as she could, 'someone has to fly you. We have a tight schedule, I believe, and we're already late. I am a pilot as well as a nurse.'

'And as irresponsible a one as I might have guessed,' he shot back at her. 'Dressing up as

Alex! What do you think this is, a kids' pantomime? I suppose you conned Miles into going along with this hare-brained scheme. I don't need to wonder why he did. You're used to twisting men around your little finger, I don't doubt. Well, not me, Sister, you won't find I'm so easy to dupe!'

Karen was incensed. His very presence made the hair on the back of her neck prickle and his insinuations riled her even more. She opened the throttle, saying as she did so, 'I hope your seat belt is securely fastened, Dr. Kendall. You're flying with a woman now!'

If he answered she did not hear. The little plane shot along the runway, gathering speed, and dust flew up around them. Karen kept her eye on the needle until the magic moment arrived and they lifted off into the clear morning air. During those last few moments she completely forgot her passenger. All her concentration was directed to lifting the plane off the ground, smoothly, safely and expertly. As they levelled out over the low hills she breathed a silent sigh of relief. The plane handled beautifully and she felt a rush of exhilaration. She turned her head briefly and was amused to see that Guy Kendall's face had gone quite white under his tan.

She said cheerfully, 'Nice day, Dr. Kendall.

Perfect weather for flying.'

There was an ominous silence and then above the drone of the engine she heard his clear clipped tones. 'I'm sorry to disappoint you, Sister Lalor, but shock tactics will make absolutely no difference to my decision. Your behaviour, if anything, only reinforces my opinion that a woman is not suitable for the job. And I shall have something to say to those you appear to have conned into organising this shabby little charade. It is totally irresponsible and reprehensible.'

Karen could only agree with that. It was, and she should not have gone along with it. She had not, however, expected him to assume that she had engineered it by using her feminity to con Miles and Alex into abetting her. So she preferred not to answer him. She kept her eyes glued to the scenery unfolding below like an architectural diorama with its miniature trees, sunbaked hills and long straight dust roads and meandering dry creek beds.

She thought to herself with a strange thrill that was something quite apart from the unpleasant man beside her, 'So this is Kendall's Kingdom!'

CHAPTER FOUR

It was strange, Karen reflected later, that in spite of the sound of the aircraft's engine, the only sensation she could recall of flying with Dr. Guy Kendall that day was total silence.

Below, seeming to stretch forever, were the vast open spaces of Kendall's Kingdom in the searing summer heat, while in the cabin was arctic silence and the oppressive iceberg presence of the man next to her, his hostility a palpable thing between them. More than once she wished she had not agreed to this lunatic enterprise. But it was too late now. She tried to put all thoughts of Dr. Kendall from her mind and concentrate on her flying and the scenery below, but every slight movement made her tense as though to resist physical aggression.

She had expected him to order her to turn the aircraft round, but once they were airborne he did not speak except to guide her to the first landing strip, which was on his own home station. She was pleased to be able to reply that she had already spotted it. Wirrumburra Downs homestead lay in the lap of low purplish-red hills dotted with scrubby trees on their lower slopes, bald on top. Several clusters of buildings nestled in a shallow valley where there were more trees and actually bright green grass. Dusty, indistinct tracks and wider roads radiated from the tiny settlement, vanishing into the hazy distance. A cloud of red dust indicated a vehicle travelling along one of them. Apart from that there was no sign of life at all, not even a sheep.

That is, until Karen had banked and turned into the wind in order to approach the graded landing strip which stood out like a rectangular strip of sticking plaster on the mottled red skin of the surrounding terrain. Wheels down and ready for the final smooth glide in, Karen suddenly saw to her horror three huge kangaroos bounding towards the airstrip. They were going to cross right in front of the plane as she touched down.

As though right inside her head she heard Dr. Kendall yell, 'Look out!' but she had seen the danger a second ahead of him, decided she could not risk landing, and with a lurch the little plane rose steeply into the air again, stirring dust up around it. Karen felt the blood drain from her face and her ears pop and she dared not look at her passenger. She circled round again. The kangaroos were still visible, bounding off into the distance. Karen's heart was pounding but she also felt a curious elation. Disaster had threatened and she had averted it. She could not have asked for a better test of her ability to act quickly in an emergency.

She glanced at Dr. Kendall but he was staring impassively at the vanishing animals.

'Damn him!' she thought, and brought the plane round for her second approach.

Now she saw that the cloud of red dust she had noticed before had halted at the edge of the landing strip and two trucks were now parked there. Using every bit of skill she possessed, Karen set the aircraft down on the strip with scarcely any sway and the lightest of bumps. The plane came to a halt at last only a few yards from the waiting trucks. Karen found that her hands were trembling. She hoped Dr. Kendall would not notice.

She need not have worried. He was already scrambling out of the aircraft, leaving her without a word. Two men in khaki shorts and wide-brimmed hats approached and two aborigines sat on the sides of one of the trucks. There was a stiff wind blowing and dust drifted in eddies across the airstrip. The sun beat down with a heat fiercer than Karen had experienced before, and even sunglasses did not completely cut out the glare. Karen grimaced to herself with a feeling of intense satisfaction. It was the first time she had ever landed on an outback airstrip. Although she had not told Dr. Kendall so, flying with Sean had meant landing at the town airfield and being driven to his parents' property by car, a very sophisticated procedure by comparison. She had certainly never had to cope with kangaroos on the runway before!

Moving swiftly, she followed Miles' instructions and knocked in the mooring pegs to hold the plane steady while they were away. She was not going to let Dr. Kendall catch her out on details if she could help it. One of the aborigines came across to help her. She straightened up to find Dr. Kendall staring impatiently back at her, his medical kit in his hand, obviously anxious to be off.

She ran across to the waiting group by the trucks.

'Hurry up, we're late,' he snapped.

'I'm sorry,' she answered, 'but we'd be worse than late if the wind turned the aircraft over while we're away.'

He just looked through her.

'Nice work,' said the older of the two men,

74

doffing his hat to Karen. 'Eh, Guy? Don't know why those dratted roos always pick the wrong moment.'

'They don't always!' said the younger man, with a grin at Karen.

Guy Kendall, unsmiling, brusquely introduced them. 'Jim Brady, Scott Brady, Sister Lalor.'

The younger man tipped his hat. 'Nice to know you, Sister.'

Karen could not see his features too clearly through her dark glasses and the hat partly shaded his face anyway, but he sounded pleasant. She presumed that the older man was his father, and that Jim Brady was Dr. Kendall's manager, although Guy seemed disinclined to enlarge on the introduction.

He said irritably, 'Let's get going, Scott, we haven't got all day.'

Karen gave him a frosty look. She would treat him as coolly as he treated her, she thought belligerently. If he had been impressed with her recent performance he clearly did not intend to show it. Whatever she did today, she thought glumly, she might as well resign herself to the fact that it was not going to make any difference. He had made up his mind and right or wrong he would not budge.

'Get in,' he barked as they skirted the rear

of the first truck.

Scott Brady was already in the driver's seat. The other truck, she noticed, carried a large drum, presumably to top up the aircraft's fuel tanks.

'I'll get in the back,' Karen offered, grasping the side of the truck.

Dr. Kendall glared at her. 'Get up in front and be quick about it. You're holding us up.'

She obeyed, heaving herself up into the cabin of the truck, not expecting and not getting any assistance from him. Foolishly she assumed that he intended to ride in the back and had shown an unexpected gallantry in allowing her to ride in front. How wrong she was!

She flopped on to the warm seat and wiped her hand across her forehead.

'Warming up today,' remarked Scott Brady, giving Karen a mildly flirtatious glance.

Before Karen could comment she was shoved roughly across the seat by Guy swinging up beside her.

'You don't need all the seat, do you?' he asked with a contemptuous look.

Karen flushed and Scott said, 'A nurse who can fly, that's a treasure, Guy. Where did you find her?'

'Let's get moving, Scott,' said Guy curtly. 'I

76

gather there's quite a crowd waiting today and there's only one doctor, remember.'

Scott, unmoved by Guy's urging, merely raised his eyebrows slightly and gave Karen a quizzical grin. He put the truck into gear, managing to brush Karen's knee in the process, and the vehicle shot forward and the dust swirled up around them.

Karen felt like a filling in a sandwich on that drive to the homestead, about two or three kilometres away. It was decidedly uncomfortable in the heat having Guy's long lean body pressed hard against her, and disconcerting, too. She could feel the boniness of his hips, and his thighs, through the light cotton trousers they were both wearing, were warm and hard against her own. The cabin of the truck was hot and stifling, but to open the windows would mean more red dust than was already filtering through. Karen's throat was dry and she longed for a cool drink.

The truck bumped along the track in a hair-raising fashion at a speed she considered reckless and she could not avoid swaying first hard against Guy and then against Scott, and all the time she was conscious of the stiff resistance of Guy's body, the relaxed acquiescence of Scott's.

Men! she thought. They're either one sort

or the other, never nice and ordinary and normal. No, she amended, Miles is nice. It was a pity that she was not attracted to Miles, really. Not that either Scott Brady or Guy Kendall attracted her, she assured herself hastily, outraged at the implication of her thoughts. Dr. Kendall she disliked intensely and Scott as just a pleasant, harmless flirt.

It was with immense relief that she saw the homestead ahead of them, appearing like an oasis as they skirted a low, gently rolling hill. The house was red-roofed and rambling, with wide verandahs covered in dark green creepers and spreading peppermint trees shading it. The truck skidded to a halt between the house and some sheds and immediately a crowd of aboriginal children darted out from everywhere to welcome them, shouting and laughing and clambering all over the vehicle, peering in at them.

Guy swung the passenger door wide. 'Hi, there, Susie, Tim,' he greeted the two clinging to the now wound-down window. He rattled off a few more names as he jumped down. Karen was surprised and touched at his kindly tone and the affectionate way he ruffled the small dark heads. It was the first sign she had seen of humanity in the man, she thought rather wryly.

'Who's the lady?' asked the little girl called Susie, smiling shyly at Karen, and showing brilliant white teeth.

'Where's Dr. Cable?' demanded another.

'This is Sister Lalor,' said Guy briskly. 'She's helping me today. Now, come on, let's go.'

Karen followed a few paces behind and a hand sneaked into each of hers. Childish voices chattered gaily, asking questions, squealing, laughing, while others skipped along beside them.

The shade of the trees was welcome and Karen's skin began to cool immediately. She followed Guy across a remarkably green lawn and up the half-dozen wooden steps to the verandah. There were groups of aborigines sitting under the trees, a few cars and trucks parked in the open space on the other side of the house, she noticed, and there was a hum of voices from the verandah. Dark faces peered at Karen curiously.

A man with crutches moved off the steps to let them through and a baby started wailing as its mother, standing at the top of the steps, rocked it to and fro and crooned soothingly to it. Somebody else was coughing in the deep shadows.

Greetings flew at them from all sides. Guy

opened the screen door and stood back for Karen to enter the house. She paused uncertainly in the wide hallway, unable to see at first in the dimness. Then she remembered her sunglasses and removed them. It was still gloomy but blessedly cool and smelled tangily of lavender polish. She glimpsed a sitting room with floral-patterned easy chairs, through a door which stood ajar on one side, but Guy was pushing open a door opposite it.

He turned to her, his eyes expressionless. 'There's a bathroom just off the bedroom. You can scrub up there. The surgery is the sleepout at the far end of the verandah. Be there in five minutes.'

Before she could open her mouth to speak he strode on through the house, leaving her to her own devices.

Karen entered the room and found it to be a large cool high-ceilinged bedroom with a big double bed in the middle and venetian blinds on the windows. It was tempting to throw herself across the ice-blue counterpane and forget what she was here for. But she was determined to go through with it now and indeed had little option.

She removed Alex's cap and battle jacket but left the scarf around her hair. She reflected with some amusement that it would be the first time she had nursed in pants and a T-shirt—and would probably be the last!

She went into the bathroom where she found fluffy white towels on a blue washbasin with blue-tiled surround, a blue-tiled shower recess and blue and white floor. It was quite luxurious. It was also vaguely masculine—Dr. Kendall's bedroom no doubt when he was at home here. She longed to snatch a quick cool shower to refresh herself but dared not. Guy had said five minutes and she had no doubt that he meant it—exactly. She sighed and thoroughly scrubbed her hands and arms and patted cool water on her face. When she returned to the bedroom there was a light tap at the door and to Karen's, 'Come in!' a woman entered.

She was middle-aged, slim and attractive and surprisingly unlined for the climate although her face was deeply tanned.

'Hello, Sister,' she greeted Karen in a friendly voice, 'I'm Jean Brady. You've already met my husband and son.' She eyed Karen smilingly. 'Mmm, Scott's right, you are the prettiest thing we've seen around here in a long time.'

Karen flushed. 'How do you do, Mrs. Brady?'

'I heard about the near miss at the strip,'

said Mrs. Brady. 'Not a nice experience on your first trip. Well, let's hope it won't happen again. I hope you're going to enjoy working with us, Sister.'

Karen was touched by the friendly manner of the manager's wife, and the way she said 'us' made it seem like one big family. A lump suddenly came into her throat because she was not going to be part of it after all—unless ... Swiftly she killed the faint hope that Guy Kendall would change his mind.

'I'm afraid I'm only standing in for Dr. Cable for today,' she confessed. 'He's unwell.'

Mrs. Brady's face fell. 'Oh! Oh, I thought you must be his replacement ... your being a pilot, I mean, as well as a nurse. Scott was saying what a bit of luck getting someone like you who can do both jobs. Guy never mentioned that Alex was sick.'

Karen glanced at her watch. 'I'd better hurry,' she said. 'I don't expect Dr. Kendall likes to be kept waiting.'

It was then she noticed the white coat Mrs. Brady was carrying. The woman held it out. 'Yes, of course. I mustn't keep you gossiping. Here ... this is bound to be a bit big for a slip of a girl like you, but you can roll up the sleeves.'

Karen slipped into it, rather surprised as she

had not thought uniforms would be strictly necessary on these trips. She belted it around her tiny waist. It reached well past her knees and she had to roll the sleeves up quite a bit. She felt rather foolish in it, but a glance in the mirror on the wardrobe door told her it didn't look as silly as it felt, and anyway if Guy ordered her to wear it, wear it she must. How like him to do things to the letter!

She reached the surgery at the end of the verandah ahead of Guy and was relieved. As she entered the sleepout her eyes flicked around the room, which had been equipped as a surgery. Open louvres down one side were screened to keep insects out and outside there was the dense greenery of a creeper. A cool breeze filtered through in spite of the heat. The room was equipped with a wash basin, a formica-topped bench and an examination couch. Dr. Kendall was a very thorough and efficient man. There was nothing makeshift about this makeshift surgery, she thought.

When he came in a moment or two later she was already laying out his stethoscope and other instruments which he might need. Again he looked steadily at her for a moment, as though weighing her up, and said nothing until, 'You can ask the first patient to come in now.'

83

The first patient was a man with a deep cut in his arm, only inflicted that morning, and very inexpertly bandaged although the bleeding had stopped. Dr. Kendall examined it and then said, 'Sister will dress it for you, Thomas.'

Suddenly Karen felt all fingers and thumbs and her throat constricted. It was nearly a year since she had given up nursing and this was hardly the perfect way to be precipitated back into it. It was not the task she had to do, that was simple enough, it was knowing that Guy Kendall was sitting there watching her every move critically and no doubt anxious to find fault.

While the patient grinned happily at her, and Guy unnecessarily rattled off what she would need and where to find it, Karen took a deep breath. With a deliberate effort of will she cleared all thoughts out of her mind except the job in hand, and it was strange, the minute she did that, second nature took over and she dealt swiftly and expertly with the patient. Guy said not another word until she had finished.

When he spoke it was only to the patient. 'Cheerio, Thomas. Take good care of that arm, won't you. You've only got two, remember.'

'Thanks, Boss,' muttered the aborigine and

sidled out with a backward grateful smile at Karen.

She felt cheered by that genuinely warm smile, curiously reassured and indeed filled with a sense of triumph out of all proportion to her achievement—or so it might seem to anyone but her. The fact was that she had started nursing again. The task had been simple enough, but to her it was a barrier crossed and she knew for certain now that she could return to the career she had so loved without the ghost of Sean dogging her. She glanced at Guy, who was writing on a file card. How he would probably deride her if he knew how mixed up her emotions had been. Cold, clinical Dr. Kendall would have no sympathy for feminine lack of logic.

Karen went to the door and called the next patient. He was a stockman with a gashed and broken finger and the accident had happened several days ago. It was now septic.

'You should have called me up,' admonished Dr. Kendall as he removed the rough splint the man had put on himself. 'That's badly infected.'

'I didn't want to fuss, Doc,' said the stockman. 'She's okay, doesn't hurt much. I thought it wouldn't matter waiting a day or two for the clinic.'

'Next time, call me up first and let me decide,' said Guy firmly.

The man grinned at Karen as she injected the antibiotic Guy had ordered. 'I guess there'll be a few folks calling you up, Doc, for a special visit now that you've got a glamorous pilot.'

Guy did not explain the temporary nature of Karen's duties and naturally neither did she. She caught his eye briefly as she withdrew the needle but he did not smile at the man's remark.

Time flew swiftly. The steady stream of patients came and went and Karen applied bandages, gave injections, soothed babies and small children, chatted to old people, listened to gossip, weighed pregnant mothers and dispensed medicines on Dr. Kendall's instructions. She became so absorbed in her duties that most of the time she forgot whom she was working with and only thought of the job.

At last she looked out on to the verandah and found it empty.

'That's the lot,' she said, and tried him with a smile. He did not respond but said:

'More patients than usual this morning. It usually is the biggest surgery here, as a few neighbours can make it to us without much trouble. I've an idea, however, that what sent a few of them in who really only came for the ride to start with was curiosity. Some very vague aches and pains around today!' He made it sound as though it was her fault.

'If we're still behind time,' she said coolly, 'then perhaps we'd better be moving right away.' She started to repack the medical kit.

'Not until after lunch,' he said brusquely, taking off his coat. 'But we'll have to cut that a bit short today in the circumstances.'

As he spoke Mrs. Brady put her head round the door. 'Lunch is ready if you are, Guy.'

'Be right there,' he answered, and Karen was again acutely aware of a warmth in his tone that was there whenever he spoke to anyone else but her. She felt irritated but knew she had only herself to blame. He believed that this morning's shoddy deception was all her idea.

As Karen went back to the bedroom to tidy herself before lunch she heard sounds of chatter and laughter and saw in the shadows beneath the trees groups of people picnicking. Clinic day at Wirrumburra Downs Station was evidently quite a social occasion. Just how social she did not realise until she finally found her way to the dining room. She had taken off the hot headscarf and had tied her coppery hair up in a pony tail for comfort and coolness. A few tendrils that would not stay inside the band fell attractively over her ears. As she came out of the bedroom, Guy was crossing the hall. He looked her over rather disconcertingly and she followed him to the dining room. She was unprepared for the dozen or so people seated around the long table. It appeared that friends and neighbours always stayed to lunch and today there was an even larger gathering than usual. All eyes focused on Karen as she entered with Guy. Most of them were male and showed appreciation.

Karen was introduced, but again Guy let everyone assume she was taking over Alex Cable's job and she thought it was hardly up to her to correct that impression. Did it mean, she asked herself cautiously, that perhaps he was going to change his mind after all? She hugged the thought to her but hardly dared entertain it seriously.

She was conscious all through the meal that Guy was also aware of the admiring glances she was receiving from the men and that he disapproved. It was hardly her fault, she thought. She did not feel attractive by any means, with no make-up, in jeans and T-shirt, and her hair tied up all anyhow. Scott Brady managed to commandeer most of her attention and since she felt she knew him as well as anyone she was glad; the crowd had suddenly made her feel rather shy.

Talk was mainly of station matters, and when Mrs. Brady brought in coffee Guy stood up and pushed his chair back. His eyes met Karen's briefly before he turned to his manager's wife and said:

'Not for us, thanks, Jean. We must be on our way. We're behind schedule already. We'll be offered a cuppa along the line somewhere, I expect.'

Somehow his tone seemed to convey that the lateness was all Karen's fault. She hurriedly gathered up her shoulder-bag and Alex's jacket and cap which she did not put on again, and was climbing into the cabin of the truck when Guy walked across to it. At least he couldn't accuse her now of holding him up.

He did not sit next to her this time in the aircraft but in one of the seats behind. Her hopes plummeted. If he would not sit next to her then obviously he did not intend to reverse his decision. However well she performed to-day, she thought miserably, it would never make up for deceiving him this morning. Again she wished she had not let Miles talk her into it, because all it was achieving was making her want more than ever to stay.

Their next stop was a mining camp with a

very rough airstrip, and Karen had a few bad moments as they touched down and slewed rather precariously across the uneven ground. There were only three patients to see and these were attended to in a corner of one of the huts, mercifully air-conditioned. Again, Karen was conscious of admiring glances from the men who came out to meet them and of Guy's tight-lipped disapproval. It puzzled her a little, since she was quite sure that Nurse Morwell must receive a similar reception and that Dr. Kendall would be used to it. Men who toiled alone in arid country such as this always welcomed a pretty female face.

Their last stop was at a station where a man was recovering from a heart attack. Guy actually vouchsafed the information that he should be in hospital but had flatly refused to go.

'It would be more than his life's worth to force him,' he said as they walked from the four-wheel drive vehicle which had brought them in from the airstrip, 'and as he's got a splendid wife, an ex-nurse, he's got a good chance of recovery.'

Mrs. Parsons was eager for a chat and as Karen was not really needed in her nursing capacity for this visit she sat at the kitchen table and talked over a cup of tea. As Guy had done so often already, she let the woman assume she was taking over from Alex Cable, as she did not feel up to giving an explanation that would only amount to a lie. It could not matter. She would never see any of these people again. The knowledge made her feel sad, as in only one day she had found affinity with the friendly, warm, outback people she had met on the stations they had visited.

As they were talking there was a knock at the door. Mrs. Parsons rose with a grimace.

'Bound to be someone for Guy. The word goes round like wildfire when he's due. I thought he was going to have an easy time today.'

She returned accompanied by a small aboriginal boy cradling a pup in his arms.

'This is Billie,' she said to Karen. 'His pup's got a broken leg. Evidently it ran under one of the horses just a while ago. He wants Guy to fix it for him.' She laughed, kindly. 'I told him Dr. Kendall isn't a vet but maybe Guy will take a look at it anyway.'

Guy strolled in. 'Ready, Sister Lalor?' he queried in his abrupt tone.

Karen stood up and Mrs. Parsons said, 'Oh, Guy, Billie wants to see you.'

Guy crossed to the boy, who was standing shyly a few paces away. 'What's the trouble,

91

young Billie?' he asked placing a large hand on the boy's head. 'That's a fine-looking pup you've got. What's his name?'

'Bindi,' said the boy.

'Hi there, Bindi,' said the doctor, stroking its head and not immediately noticing the limp paw. The pup licked his fingers and whimpered. At that, Guy examined him more closely.

'Bindi's broke 'is leg,' said Billie. 'I want you to fix him up, Doc.'

For a moment Karen thought, as Guy glanced at his watch, that he was not going to take the time, but instead he glanced at her, almost smiled and said, 'No point in calling the vet in, is there Sister Lalor, now we're here?'

'No, Dr. Kendall,' she replied, and for a brief moment there was a glimmer of understanding between them. In that moment Karen almost liked him.

When the pup's paw had been set and encased in plaster and Mrs. Parsons had promised to look after it in her kitchen, Karen and Dr. Kendall eventually left the homestead. The jubilant Billie clung to the jeep all the way back to the airstrip. Karen caught herself regretting that she would not be coming back to see the pup frolicking around with his young master, the injured leg whole again.

Impulsively, as she fastened her seat belt, she turned around and said to Guy, 'Dr. Kendall, have you found any fault with my performance today?'

He eyed her narrowly. 'No,' he admitted grudgingly.

'And there was the hazard of the kangaroos. I coped with that, didn't I?'

'Yes,' he acknowledged in the same tone.

'Nothing wrong with my reflexes, was there?'

'No, nothing wrong with your reflexes,' he answered laconically.

'Then surely you must agree that I can cope with the job as well as a man,' she burst out in exasperation, at the same time calling herself a fool for even wanting to work with this arrogant, overbearing man should she be able to change his mind.

'I don't see anything of the kind.' His face was granite.

As his cool implacability hardened still further so her temper flared more furiously. Swiftly she reminded herself that it was her own fault for starting the conversation. With an effort of will she made herself say calmly, 'Dr. Kendall, I apologise for this morning's deception. On reflection I would really rather not have been a party to it ... it was silly and impulsive ...' She did not tell him that it had not been her idea but Miles', because that might make it worse for Miles and since she had acquiesced she was really as much to blame.

'Second thoughts are too late in real emergencies,' he said flatly. 'This job calls for clear thinking, not impulsive or hasty action or the tomfoolery you appear to be capable of.'

'I was only thinking of Alex,' she said, although that had not been wholly true. She could hardly tell him how strong was her desire to prove him wrong about her. 'He's very keen to get away and as he's already cabled his fiancée she's going to be very disappointed. Surely you could let me do the job until you find someone ... more suitable.' She laid heavy emphasis on the last words.

His eyes sparked. 'Sister Lalor, if you think you can twist me round your little finger the way you evidently did Miles and Alex, and no doubt, given the chance, you would seduce every male who eyed you off today, you are barking up the wrong tree. The answer was no yesterday and it's still no.' His eyes held hers and she knew she had never had a chance. He went on crisply, 'And now, if you don't mind, we will return to Wirrumburra instead of sitting here arguing.' He glanced pointedly at his watch.

Karen suddenly could not prevent herself letting fly. 'You are stubborn and unreasonable and what's more a male chauvinist pig!' she shouted above the roar of the engine. She was close to tears with anger and frustration and wishing now she had not swallowed her pride and begged him like that. Oh, how she hated the man!

She practically hurled the aircraft into the air. The blood was pounding in her temples and she felt an uncontrollable desire to take Dr. Guy Kendall and shake him hard, to shake some sense into him. It was just as well she had the flying to concentrate on or she might have attempted it.

It was probably that very desire that gave her the idea which once planted began to grow swiftly in her mind. Recklessly she resolved to have revenge on Dr. Kendall. It was silly and childish but she could not help it. Maybe it was a combination of red hair, Irish ancestry and her own natural impetuosity that made her do it, she reflected afterwards.

They were only a few minutes away from Wirrumburra when she quite suddenly let the aircraft drop a few hundred metres just as though they had hit a severe air pocket. A sharp exclamation from behind her made her smile as she levelled out.

'Bit of turbulence,' she shouted over her shoulder. 'Hold tight!'

She gave him half a minute to recover and then went into a dive, rocked the plane crazily, banked, dived and did every manoeuvre she had ever learned short of looping the loop. She knew it was irresponsible but the devil in her would not let her stop.

She hurled the little plane around the sky, giving him, she hoped, a few minutes of the most giddy uncertainty he had ever experienced. With his lack of faith in a woman pilot he was probably convinced she was going to kill him.

Finally she levelled out and shouted over her shoulder, 'Okay, relax, we're through it, I think.' She did not really believe she had fooled him and she did not really want to. She wanted him to know that she had done it on purpose. She glanced over her shoulder.

His eyes met hers, coldly and accusingly. But it was not his eyes that made her smile. It was his face. It had gone a whitish green colour. She turned away and the astonishing sound of Dr. Kendall being sick into a paper bag was immensely satisfying. She shook with silent laughter.

The moment the plane taxied to a halt at

Wirrumburra airfield, he flung open the door and leapt out. She watched him stride towards his car and reflected with satisfaction that he was not likely to forget her in a hurry now.

And she would not forget him, she thought, reminded suddenly of his long lean body pressed against hers in the truck, his dark steely eyes meeting hers in a glimmer of understanding, just that once, before he had set the pup's leg. Somewhere, under that arrogant, pig-headed, super-efficient and chilly exterior there must be a real man. It was a pity she would never have the chance to find him.

CHAPTER FIVE

By the time Karen left the aircraft, Dr. Guy
Kendall was just a ball of red dust bowling
along the road from the airfield. The momentary triumph she had felt suddenly evaporated
and she felt ashamed. What she had done was
silly, childish and petulant, not to mention
dangerous. A feeling of deep depression
washed over her and she could barely raise a
smile as Miles approached from the airfield
building.

He looked at her anxiously, 'Well, how did
it go?'

She shook her head numbly. 'Terrible!'

He took her arm, walking her towards the
car, his own she noticed without a glimmer
of amusement. He must have seen the way
Guy had stalked off.

'What happened? You obviously didn't
crash the plane!'

'Oh, no problems there and I found I hadn't
forgotten my nursing either.' She slid a wry
glance in his direction as she recalled. 'Although

nothing very arduous was expected of me, I have to admit.'

'Well, surely he's now convinced ...'

Karen stopped him. 'My competency today didn't mean a thing to him. Deceiving him just made matters worse. I suppose we should have known it would, Miles. Guy is not a person you trifle with.'

Miles stretched his lips grimly. 'No, I guess not.' He squeezed her arm. 'Oh, well, it was worth a try, though, wasn't it?'

'I'm not sure it was,' said Karen slowly. The feeling inside her was that she would rather not have lived through today. Something about it all had got to her. The vast open spaces, the brazen sky, the people she had met—even Guy Kendall—all of them represented a challenge and a challenge was what she most needed at this moment in her life. She crushed the thoughts. That challenge was not going to be in Kendall's Kingdom.

'You look a bit whacked,' said Miles as he opened the car door for her. 'What about a drink? Then you can go home to Ma Carson's and shower and I'll take you out to dinner.' He laughed. 'We don't run to French restaurants up here, so it'll have to be either the Club again or the hotel.'

Karen felt suddenly weary. 'Thanks, Miles,

she murmured gratefully. A long cool drink was inviting, so was a shower. Dinner she did not feel ready to face yet, but perhaps she would be hungrier after she had freshened up. It was no good regretting what had happened. Tomorrow it would all be history. With an effort she pulled herself together.

'What did he say when he discovered it was you and not Alex?' Miles asked eagerly as they left the airfield. 'I wish I'd been there to see his face!'

Karen knew he would pester her until she told him the details of the day, so she related it all from the beginning. When she came to the final row with Guy and her impulsive revenge, she hesitated, unwilling to tell Miles about it because she felt so ashamed, but in the end she did.

He roared with laughter. 'You didn't! You little devil!' He braked outside the Wirrum-burra Hotel and turned to hug Karen. 'How absolutely glorious! Guy airsick! He'll never live that down!'

Karen was alarmed. 'Miles, you won't tell anyone, please?'

He gave her a sharp look. 'Why not? He's humiliated you, so why shouldn't you get your own back? It might just teach him a lesson.'

'No, Miles.' Her tone was emphatic.

He shrugged. 'Okay. I won't breathe a word.'

They walked into the lounge of the hotel and its coolness was balm to Karen's hot face. She slumped into one of the big comfortable cane chairs and Miles sat opposite her.

'Beer?' he asked.

'Shandy, please.'

The drinks came icy cold and frosted on the outside of the glasses. Karen ran her finger-tips idly through the moisture.

Miles said, 'I'm sorry, Karen. It was a lousy idea. I shouldn't have talked you into it. I can see you're rather upset now.'

She glanced up. 'Don't start apologising again, please, Miles. I didn't have to do it. I admit I wanted to show him I could do the job. I ought to have known, too, that it was unlikely he'd give in to that sort of pressure. I ... I just wish I hadn't given in to that stupid impulse to pay him back. It was so childish.'

'Well, I certainly wouldn't worry about what Guy thinks,' said Miles.

Karen, however, in spite of herself, still wished that she had not given Dr. Kendall real grounds to regard her as irresponsible.

Miles was still smiling about it. 'It served him right. Guy airsick!' He chuckled.

As he did so the door to the lounge was

pushed inwards and he glanced up.

'Oho,' he said warningly, 'here comes our hero now. I guess he wants some soda water to settle his tummy!'

Karen's heart raced as she clasped her fingers together to stop them from trembling. Surreptitiously she glanced in the direction of the doorway. She saw not just Guy coming in but also Terri Lawson. No doubt that was why he had been in a hurry to get back on time, a date with his girlfriend. Dr. Guy Kendall had other kinds of dedication, Karen thought wryly, and Terri obviously was not the kind of girl who cared for being kept waiting.

They did not appear to notice her and Miles and Karen prayed they would not. The lounge was very crowded, however, with few empty seats, and Terri was scanning the whole room looking for somewhere to sit. She looked very cool and glamorous in a pastel blue sundress which set off her glowing suntan and blonde hair. Guy rested a hand on one of her smoothly rounded bare shoulders and Karen saw his lips move as he murmured something close to her ear. He was frowning slightly. His pallor had gone and he showed no sign of the recent air-sickness. Not that she would have expected him to. Airsickness tended to vanish immediately one was on terra firma again.

The pair turned in their search for seats and momentarily Guy's eyes seemed to fix on Karen's. She glanced away quickly and when she glanced back, to her great relief, Guy was plucking at Terri's arm, and saying something again, presumably that they would go elsewhere. However, at that moment Terri spotted the two empty seats at the table where Miles and Karen were sitting. By the enthusiastic way she pointed them out and began to drag Guy across, weaving between the tables, she could have no idea what had happened today.

'Watch out,' muttered Miles between his teeth, 'they're coming this way. I was hoping they hadn't seen us.'

'Hello, Miles,' trilled Terri, with a beaming smile. She glanced at Karen. 'Hello ... Karen, isn't it?' The slight hesitation as she pretended, Karen felt sure, to be doubtful of her name was surely meant to show her how unimportant she was.

Karen nodded. 'Hello,' she said, not using Terri's name at all, but not quite managing to give the impression she had forgotten it, as she would have liked.

Her eyes met Guy's, hard as the iron ore that abounded in his kingdom. His nostrils flared very slightly and there was a faint twitch at the corner of his mouth as he looked coldly down at her. 'Good evening, Sister Lalor,' he murmured. 'Hello, Miles.'

Terri raised one carefully shaped eyebrow. 'Guy, darling, you are formal!'

He did not answer but pulled a chair out for her and then sat down himself. Terri's full-skirted dress flounced over the arms of her chair and rose fractionally above her knees so that her long shapely legs, elegantly crossed, were seen to their best advantage. Karen noticed Guy's gaze drifting idly from her knees to the red-tipped toenails peeping from Terri's flimsy blue sandals.

Miles beckoned the steward over. 'What are you having?' he asked the newcomers.

Guy ordered beer and Terri a martini. As she sipped it daintily, twirling the olive on its toothpick in elegantly manicured fingers, she said rather too sweetly, 'What a shame you didn't pass your test today, Karen. Still, I wouldn't cry over it. Guy's a very tough taskmaster, aren't you, darling?' She shot an admiring glance at him, sitting stony-faced, both hands clasped around his glass of beer, staring moodily into it, and went on, 'And the job really does need someone exceptional.'

Karen seethed but controlled the burst of

anger she felt like delivering.

Miles, however, was incensed on her behalf. 'I gather Karen was not the only one not to pass her test,' he said drily with a knowing grin at Guy, who had raised his eyes at the remark. His glance slid from Miles to Karen, eyes slightly narrowed and showing a momentary flicker of discomfort as he waited for her to reveal with malicious glee that he had been airsick.

Karen resisted the impulse to mock him in front of Terri. She said calmly, 'Is it always as hot up here as it was today?'

Guy's features relaxed perceptibly. 'Sometimes it's even hotter,' he answered. He was still looking at her face, a new look now, part surprise and part speculation. Possibly he was wondering why she had not spoken about his airsickness: she was wondering why herself.

Fortunately Terri did not follow up Miles's cryptic remark and it drifted into oblivion. She uncrossed and re-crossed her legs and with a smile handed her glass to the hovering steward. Then she said, 'I really don't know how anyone can stand it all year round, even with air-conditioning. It's like spending your life popping in and out of a refrigerator.'

'You don't live up here all year round?' Karen inquired.

Terri laughed. 'Heavens, no! I go south whenever I can, especially in summer. We have a beach house and at least there's a bit of real life down there. It is pretty deadly here.'

Miles put in. 'It isn't very sophisticated, to be sure, but we do have a weekly dance, barbecues, tennis, cricket and football as well as other sports.'

'Ugh!' exclaimed Terri, who was evidently no sportswoman. 'How anyone could bear to play tennis in this heat I can't imagine.'

'Doesn't hurt you to have a good sweat occasionally,' said Miles bluntly.

Terri smiled sweetly at him. 'Thank you, darling, I'd rather just gently perspire on the sidelines.'

Guy rose, looking at his watch. 'Come along, Terri, time we went. The Luscombes will be wondering what has happened to us.'

Terri stood up. She gave Karen a condescending look. 'Well, goodbye, Karen. Nice to have met you. I hope you have better luck with the next position you apply for.' Her insincerity was cloaked in a smile that was no more than a brief rearrangement of her features.

Karen murmured, 'Thank you. Goodbye.' She glanced at Guy. 'Goodbye, Dr. Kendall.'

He studied her coolly for a moment. 'Good-bye, Sister,' he said at last, but added no good wishes for her future as even Terri had done. Not that she blamed him for that. How he must hate her! She had amply justified his decision not to let her stay.

As they left and Miles subsided back into his chair, he said, 'Well, if you've finished your drink, Karen, we might as well go, too. I expect you're dying for a shower.'

She nodded. 'I am. I feel very grubby. But thanks, Miles, for the drink. I needed that, too.'

Depression settled even more heavily over Karen as she showered and changed. She wore a pale pink and green floral cotton dress which made her look younger than her years. Mrs. Carson chatted to her while she was waiting for Miles and Karen told her a little about Linda.

'I hope she isn't too flighty,' said Ma Carson anxiously. Karen wondered if she considered her flighty as a result of this morning's episode in dressing gown and bare feet.

'No, Linda's not flighty,' she assured the landlady, although wondering if in Ma Carson's book that description might not fit the irrepressible Linda. Of course Linda might change her mind about coming at all now that Karen was not going to be there. Karen again wondered if she ought to change *her* mind and stay for Linda's sake, but the thought of it made her shudder. She just couldn't, not even for Linda.

When Miles tooted the car horn, Karen picked up her handbag and went down the garden path to meet him.

Despite Miles' cheery conversation, his amusing hospital stories, Karen's mood would not lighten. She longed for tomorrow and escape. It had been a dreadful fiasco and she dreaded having to tell her parents about it, as well as the unsuspecting Linda.

The following morning Karen had just finished her shower when she again heard voices in the hall as she was leaving the bathroom, clutching her robe around her loosely. The man's voice this time was Alex Cable's. She was surprised because Miles had said he would call for her and drive her to the airfield to catch the plane south. It seemed that Alex was calling in his place, but it was much earlier than Miles had said. Whether Ma Carson approved or not scarcely mattered now, so Karen tiptoed along to the sitting room in her bare feet and looked in.

'Good morning, Alex,' she said brightly. 'I'm not ready yet. I wasn't expecting ...'

108

'Hi, Karen!' He grinned at her. He seemed quite cheered up for some reason.

'I was expecting Miles,' Karen said, puzzled, 'but not for a couple of hours yet. What's up?'

Ma Carson's lips pursed slightly as she observed Karen's flimsy attire once again. She faded diplomatically into the background but seemed disinclined to leave them alone together. Alex's next words came as a shock to Karen.

'Guy wants a word with you, Karen.'

'Dr. Kendall wants a word with *me*!' Karen was flabbergasted and her throat went dry. 'Why? There can't be anything he wants to say to me now.'

Alex shrugged. 'He seems to think there is. He told me to tell you he wants a word before you leave.'

Before she left. As Karen's mind repeated the words she knew that for one crazy second she had hoped he had changed his mind. As if he would! All he wanted was to have the last word, she thought, to tear a strip off her for her behaviour yesterday, possibly even to threaten to report her to the authorities, perhaps scare her into thinking she could lose her licence because of if ... All sorts of mad possibilities entered her head, none of which was very plausible, but paramount was the thought that whatever it was he wanted to say, she was not going to listen to it.

'Well, I'm not going to ...' she began hotly, then aware of Ma Carson standing curiously by, she calmed down and said, 'I really don't see that it's necessary.'

'He probably only wants to give you your pay for yesterday,' suggested Alex.

Karen snorted. 'Now you have to be joking!'

'Karen, it won't hurt just to see what he wants,' said Alex, 'and you'll still have plenty of time to catch your plane.'

She supposed he would suffer if he failed to persuade her to go. She bit her lip. 'All right,' she said reluctantly. 'I won't be long.'

'I'll wait.' Alex grinned at Ma Carson. 'Got any girlie mags lying around, Ma, to amuse me while I'm waiting?'

'Certainly not!' exclaimed Ma Carson but Karen saw the smile in her eyes.

'Never mind, I'll thumb through the *Women's Weekly* instead,' said Alex amiably, lowering his large frame into a big armchair and reaching for the top one of a pile of magazines on a table beside him. 'The lingerie ads are nearly as good!'

Karen fled. There was absolutely no reason why she should subject herself to scalding words from Dr. Kendall, she thought rebelliously as she brushed her hair, no reason at all. She would change her mind and not go. But at the same time she could not help wondering what he did want to say to her, and worse, she could not help wanting one last glimpse of that steely-eyed, arrogant, thoroughly unpleasant medico.

Nurse Morwell smiled pleasantly at Karen as she walked in with Alex.

'Oh, Dr. Cable,' she said. 'Dr. Kendall said would you take Sister Lalor straight along to his office.'

Karen's knees felt wobbly but she steeled herself for the confrontation and determined it would be brief. She had already rehearsed how she was going to control the interview.

Alex Cable opened the door to the office and held it wide.

'Go in,' he said to Karen. 'I'll be waiting outside.'

Karen felt a little like a prisoner going to her execution as she entered the white-walled room. She let her eyes drift over the shelves of medical books, the colourful modern paintings, and out of the window to the leafy garden beyond. A spray of scarlet poinciana brushed the glass and as her gaze reached the desk, the cane armchair beside it, the polished oak floor, she realised he was not there. She moved towards the chair, intending to sit down and wait, and as she did so his voice came from behind and to the right of her.

'Good morning, Sister Lalor.'

She wheeled. He was standing near a small table which had been out of her range of vision as she had opened the door. He was looking at slides through a microscope. This morning his deep tan stood out in stark contrast with the white hospital coat and his dark hair was shining and sleek, brushed back from the slight widow's peak at the centre of his forehead. His fingertips drummed lightly on the table top as he stood looking steadily at her, not speaking. She found her own eyes fixed not on his face but on the fuzz of dark hairs on his forearms below the rolled-up sleeves.

He moved away from the table towards her. Karen stood rooted to the floor. Her earlier bravado seemed to have deserted her and her throat was dry with nervous anticipation. Momentarily he stood very close to her, looking down at her with that hard uncompromising look she already knew well, until she felt compelled to meet his gaze.

When she did so he said rather drily, 'Good of you to come, Sister.' He walked over to his desk, again standing in characteristic fashion with the splayed fingers of both hands gently piano-playing imaginary scales on the polished wood. 'Please sit down,' he said.

Karen, however, recovered some of her composure and remained standing. She took a deep breath. 'I'm sure that what you have to say to me, Dr. Kendall, cannot take long, so as Dr. Cable is waiting for me perhaps you would be good enough to tell me what you called me here for. I am sure you do not want me to miss my plane.' She tilted her chin challengingly as she took another deep breath before going on. He opened his mouth to speak but before he did so she plunged into her rehearsed speech. 'I feel I must apologise for the turbulence of yesterday which was not entirely due to the atmosphere, as I am sure you are aware. It was a spur-of-the-moment prank because you provoked me, and I sincerely regret any ... any inconvenience it caused you.' That, she thought, will take the wind out of his sails. He can hardly upbraid me now I've apologised.

His face was quite impassive as she delivered her speech, showing neither surprise nor mollification. His dark eyes seemed to pin her, she felt, like some botanical specimen, to the wall behind. Then unexpectedly he burst out laughing. He said, 'For God's sake, Karen, sit down!'

He slumped into his own swivel chair, twirling it back and forth, but she still remained standing.

'I have a plane to catch,' she again reminded him icily.

'Like hell you have,' he said. 'Sit down!' It was a voice that commanded obedience, and Karen, in spite of herself, moved to the chair and sat. She perched on the edge, and waited for him to speak again.

He leaned one elbow on the arm of his chair and rested his chin against his palm as he regarded her with a curious little smile. 'I've changed my mind,' he said bluntly. 'You can stay.'

Karen felt as though she was going to faint. She simply could not be hearing him say that. He was not the kind of man to change his mind, especially after what she had done to him ...

'What?' she muttered stupidly.

'Unless you're stone deaf I imagine that you heard me,' he said.

She was thoroughly perplexed. 'But ... why?'

A tentative smile lifted the corners of his mouth. 'Perhaps because I am not as stubborn and unreasonable as you appear to believe. I adhere to my belief that it's no job for a woman, let alone a slip of a girl like you, but as Alex is so lovesick I can't afford to have him running out at a moment's notice and leaving us in the lurch.'

Karen felt anger rising in her. How dared he push her about from pillar to post just to suit himself? Why couldn't he have seen it this way yesterday? And why couldn't he have changed his mind because of her competence, not for Alex's convenience?

Incensed anew, she rose from the chair saying, 'If that's your only reason for changing your mind, Dr. Kendall, I'm afraid I don't want the job now, thank you very much. I wouldn't work for you for all the ... all the iron in Kendall's Kingdom! You are arrogant and rude and you think you can manipulate everyone who comes within your orbit just as you choose. You might be king around here, Dr. Kendall, but don't count me among your subjects! No, I am not changing *my* mind!'

She strode angrily towards the door. Before her hand reached the knob she felt a grip of iron on her upper arm and she was turned roughly to face him, her body only inches from his, his eyes boring into hers, a strangely intense expression on his face.

'Yesterday,' he said calmly, 'it was you who said you had acted for Alex's sake. Your concern for him was very fleeting, very superficial, was it not? Or do you always put yourself first in the end?'

Fury almost choked her. He was a devil this man, twisting words and actions to suit himself. She held his gaze stonily, resisting.

His grip on her arm tightened. 'Well?' he demanded. 'Are you going to let him down? He's counting on you. He doesn't imagine for a minute that you are fickle. He thinks you really wanted the job.'

Her resolve faltered. She saw Alex Cable's morose face when Miles had given him the bad news. He was in love, anxious to go home to New Zealand to be with his fiancée, to get married. And it was perfectly true that she had wanted the job, until this minute. She knew she was trapped now. Dr. Kendall had outsmarted her after all, not in any way she could have anticipated but totally by surprise. He had climbed down, it was true, but she, by throwing it back in his face, had turned the tables on herself. Fury with him struggled with the desire not to disappoint Alex and in the end her better nature won over her pride.

'All right,' she muttered through clenched teeth, 'I'll stay.'

He smiled now, a smug smile of victory, and released her. She staggered slightly, aware of a stinging sensation on her arm where he had gripped her.

'Now come back and sit down and we'll discuss a few details,' he said matter-of-factly and with the air of never having argued with her at all.

She meekly followed and sank into the chair, a glance out of the corner of her eye showing her a spread mark where his fingers had encircled her arm.

'But Alex is waiting,' she protested at once.

'Of course he isn't,' said Dr. Kendall.

Karen opened her mouth in surprise. 'You mean you told him you were going to ask me to stay?' She remembered Alex's more cheerful look this morning and understood it now. 'Why didn't he tell me?'

'Perhaps he thought you might be a little, shall we say ... truculent?' He smiled infuriatingly and she knew he had expected her outburst and had told Alex not to tell her because he was afraid she might refuse to see him.

So he had made up his mind before her apology, she thought, irrelevantly because it did not alter the situation one bit to know that. She stared at his bent head as he extracted a folder from a drawer and wondered how on earth, now she had committed herself, she was going to tolerate working with this abominable man. There were bound to be fireworks.

CHAPTER SIX

At Alex Cable's farewell party it seemed that the whole of Wirrumburra and a few more besides were crammed into the Wirrumburra Club, Karen danced most of the evening with Miles and Alex as she still knew few people outside the hospital.

'I don't believe I've thanked you, Karen,' Alex said the first time they shuffled around the crowded floor together.

'Thanked me?' she queried. 'Whatever for?'

'Well, if it hadn't been for you, I wouldn't be flying out tomorrow.'

She laughed ruefully. 'You know very well I'm not responsible for that. Guy Kendall just took pity on you.' She shook her finger playfully at him, 'And don't forget who plotted to try and make him!'

Alex nodded and said with a laugh, 'Well, it worked! Although you must have given him good reason to change his mind about you. He must have been very impressed. He wouldn't have done it just to suit me.'

Karen felt the colour rising in her cheeks as she recalled that hectic buzzing around the sky with Guy probably convinced his last moments had come. It seemed that Miles had kept his word and not mentioned it to anyone, not even Alex. It really was extraordinary that Dr. Kendall had changed his mind after she had done that to him. She still couldn't understand it.

She said, 'Somehow I don't think Dr. Kendall's mind works with quite the same logic as other people's.'

Alex chuckled. 'You could be right. He's a hard man to know, seldom lets his hair down and never looks relaxed. I beg your pardon ... expect perhaps right now!'

Karen followed his gaze and saw Guy dancing with Terri Lawson. She was talking animatedly and his eyes were on her face, fixed on her mouth as though it fascinated him. His own lips were slightly twisted in a sensuous half smile. Perhaps he was anticipating kissing her, Karen thought, which no doubt he often did. She felt faintly embarrassed at allowing such an intimate speculation.

Alex said, 'Since Eileen isn't here I can say it—Terri's certainly a smasher. Guy knows how to pick 'em.' He glanced at Karen. 'Maybe that's why he changed his mind about you.'

She was perplexed. 'I don't know what you mean.'

He grinned. 'Competition for the glamorous Terri in case she's getting ideas he doesn't want her to, yet.'

'Well, hardly.'

Alex laughed. 'Nevertheless, you'd better watch out, Karen.'

Whether she should watch out for Guy or Terri, Karen was not quite sure, but she was sure that Dr. Kendall had not changed his mind simply because he liked the look of her. He was not a man to mix his private life with hospital business. Nevertheless the thought dangled in her mind—was Guy Kendall the kind of man Alex had suggested?

Miles gave her a quite different kind of warning, and one that she was more inclined to heed, even though at first that seemed as ludicrous as Alex's surmise.

'Watch your step with Guy,' Miles said seriously. 'Who knows what revenge he's cooking up for you because of that little escapade in the sky?'

Startled, she said, 'Miles, you can't really think that's why he ...'

Miles shrugged. 'You dealt a severe blow to his ego that day even if no one else but you, me and he knows about it. He has a lot of personal and professional pride and you dared to dent it.'

'But, Miles, surely he'd rather be rid of me if he's afraid I might talk.'

'Oh, I don't think he's afraid of that. You didn't that night in front of Terri and Alex. And now the story has lost its sting anyway, but don't underestimate him. He's as human as the rest of us and you could be in for a rough time of it.'

'It sounds *in*human,' Karen murmured. 'Would he really be so petty?'

Again Miles shrugged. 'I don't know Guy all that well. Nobody does.'

Karen had become quickly aware of that during the first two days of her indoctrination into the routine of Wirrumburra Hospital. Dr. Kendall was respected and liked, but with certain reservations. The other nurses, even the ebullient Kelly Maguire, seemed to be in awe of him and even Matron mentioned him with a kind of deference, Karen thought, that one usually reserved for royalty. His aloof, rather cool and enigmatic manner was however perhaps just typical of men dedicated to their work.

'He may have let me stay simply to do Alex a favour,' she said. It was the reason he had given her and it was the reason she preferred to believe.

'He may,' conceded Miles, sounding unconvinced.

Karen was disturbed by both Alex's and Miles' hints that her remaining at Wirrumburra after all might not be as straightforward as it had at first seemed. She had thought it was because Dr. Kendall always put the good of others and the community before himself. She wanted to believe that but the thought lingered, what if at some time when she least expected it, Guy revenged himself? But how? That was the trouble. She had not the remotest idea what kind of humiliation he might plan for her.

Suddenly she wished she had stuck to her guns and left as she had wanted to, but seeing Alex's happy face grinning at her as he passed, she could not help feeling glad she had done the right thing by him. In the morning he would be flying to Perth. From there he would fly on to New Zealand, to Wellington, where his fiancée waited.

She sighed, envying him, and yet there was no pain. There was still an ache but she could think of Sean at last without the once familiar lurching of her heart, the yawning emptiness in the pit of her stomach. Sean was now a memory to be savoured with deep affection but without bitterness and regret, only with remembered love. She had Miles to thank for what was happening to her, in a way, Karen thought, but she must be careful that she did not let gratitude delude her into thinking that what she now felt for him was love.

She knew deep in her heart that she did not love Miles, not in the way she had loved Sean. Probably she would never love anyone again like that. There would have to be a miracle for that to happen.

The change in her, she knew very well, was not all due to Miles. She had been on the point of being cured when he came along. He had been the catalyst that had lifted her out of her long slough of despair. There were still scars but they were healing fast now.

The party was half over before Guy Kendall, suave and satorially elegant in white jacket, black trousers and a plum-coloured shirt with toning tie, loomed before Karen and asked her to dance. She had not expected him to at all in view of their strained relationship and was therefore surprised and a little nervous. Most of his attention had been devoted to Terri during the evening, but the girl was nowhere to be seen at the moment, Karen ascertained from a swift glance around the crowd behind Dr. Kendall.

Karen was not altogether sure she would enjoy the close proximity that his style of dancing demanded, but she could hardly do otherwise than drift into his arms and let herself move in rhythm with the music. His grasp was firm and his hand warm in hers. Although he smiled in a friendly enough fashion she still felt edgy.

During her first two days at the hospital she had seen little of him. Most of her time had been spent either with Matron or Nurse Kelly Maguire, who had shown her the ropes and helped her find her feet. Karen was not at all surprised to find that the hospital was run very efficiently on precision lines and that nurses, doctors and patients all seemed to jump to attention for Dr. Kendall.

'I hope you're settling in all right,' he said now, his eyes questioning. 'Matron seems to think you are very adaptable.'

Karen's mouth twitched. His tone suggested that he still needed to be convinced of her abilities. Adaptable was hardly a glowing compliment and she wondered if Matron had used that exact word. She had got along very well with Matron Muriel Fawkes right from the word go, and it would have been just like her to try to put in a good word for Karen with the redoubtable Dr. Kendall. She had, after all, joined in Miles' conspiracy on the day of the clinic.

'I like it very much,' Karen said sincerely in reply to his question and meeting his gaze boldly. 'You run a very smooth hospital, Dr. Kendall.'

His mouth twitched. 'You say that in a tone of disapproval.'

'Do I? I beg your pardon. I've no fault to find with well-oiled machinery.'

There was a slight pause, then he said, 'Your friend ... the other nurse Miles engaged. She arrives next week?'

'Yes. She couldn't come any earlier because she had to give notice where she is now.'

'I know, I know. What's her name again?'

'Linda Walters.'

'Hm, yes. You will enjoy having your friend to work beside you?'

'Certainly.'

'She didn't join you, however, when you left nursing to become a secretary?'

'There was no reason why she should,' Karen answered, aware that he was taking the opportunity to get at her.

The conversation was unbearably stilted. In the silence after the last exchange Karen searched for some innocuous topic to introduce, something as far removed from herself and nursing as possible, but found her mind a total blank.

So they moved around the floor in silence and Karen was more uncomfortable with Guy Kendall than with any other man before. Never had she been in such close contact with a man whose attraction she could not deny and yet whom she utterly detested.

In spite of herself, she kept remembering that revealing moment with the puppy and the anxious little aboriginal boy. Guy had been kind and thoughtful with all his patients, but it had been in that moment with the pup that she had seen real tenderness. It was not that he was sentimental about animals, she felt sure, it was simply that his compassion knew no bounds. And more than that, for a moment she had glimpsed another Guy Kendall, the man she could like as well as admire. It was a glimpse she felt certain she would never have again.

He said, 'How are you getting along with Ma Carson?'

Karen suspected he had been racking his brains, too, for something to say to her.

'Very well,' she answered. 'She's very kind and used to nurses and their odd hours. No gentlemen in the rooms, mind!' She mimicked

Ma Carson with a laugh and then blushed and wished she had not repeated that particular rule of her landlady's.

Dr. Kendall actually laughed, too. 'She pretends to be very prim but it's only a front because she doesn't want flighty young nurses thinking they can run rings around her. Actually, they usually do, up to a point. She's a good sort, Ella Carson, and feels responsible for the girls who stay with her. She'd do anything for anybody if they asked her.'

Once they came close to Alex, who was dancing with Terri. The look that Terri drove into Karen was lethal. Clearly she did not like to see another woman dancing with her man. Karen recalled Alex's warning and momentarily wondered if there might be some truth in what he had said. Terri and Alex swirled away and Karen saw Terri laugh into Alex's face as though trying to tell Guy she didn't care.

Karen had learned a little about Terri Lawson from Kelly Maguire. Her parents owned a sheep station adjoining Wirrumburra Downs, but her mother had not been well for years and spent most of her time down south. Terri had been educated in the city and made no secret of the fact that was where she preferred to be.

'Terri spends most of her time down south with her mother,' Kelly had said. 'She's only hanging around up here because of Guy. She's made up her mind to hook him, I'm sure, but whether he could tear himself away from here, as he'd have to if he married her, I don't know.' She sighed enviously. 'There are some women that men will do anything for!'

Karen could only agree that Terri, with her soft blonde looks and glamorous figure and expensive clothes and air of elegance, was one of them.

Kelly had added archly, 'Mind you, Guy likes playing the field. Every good-looking woman who turns up in town and isn't married usually has at least one date with Dr. Kendall.'

Karen was surprised. 'He finds the time?'

Kelly laughed. 'He might be a workaholic, but what man can't find the odd moment for a woman?' She grinned impishly. 'You'd better look out, Karen. You've got the looks to tempt him!'

'Heaven forbid!' Karen exclaimed. Privately she thought that a date with Dr. Kendall would hardly be flattering. It sounded as though one would be slotted in between operations and clinics like a hastily grabbed meat pie and coffee, to be devoured at speed without savouring.

Now he cut into her thoughts. 'Do you find it rather warm in here?'

Karen jerked back to reality. 'Oh ... er ... well, it is rather, I suppose. Perhaps the air-conditioning isn't working properly. There are a lot of people in a small space.'

She half expected him to excuse himself while he got someone to see to the air-conditioning, but he surprised her by saying, 'Shall we see if the crush is a little less out on the verandah?'

It was more like an order than an invitation, and Karen found herself being propelled around the perimeter of the dancers and towards the open french windows before she could utter a protest. They emerged on to a wide bougainvillea-shrouded verandah. There were tables and chairs there and a few couples either sitting at them or standing around leaning on the railings looking out across the Club lawns. A sprinkler turning slowly on the lawn, the flung droplets catching sparks of light, cooled the atmosphere.

'I'll get you a drink,' Guy said.

'Thank you,' Karen murmured. 'Just a bitter lemon or a dry ginger ale would be fine.'

'Don't go away,' he said, as though he thought she might. 'I'll be right back.'

He guided her to a chair in a dim corner and then disappeared. When he had not returned after nearly ten minutes she began to wonder if perhaps this was his idea of revenge, to stand her up. No, that was lacking the finesse she would expect from Dr. Guy Kendall. A moment later, to her relief, he returned.

'Terrible crush at the bar,' he apologised. 'They were out of bitter lemon, so it's dry ginger.'

'That's fine, thanks,' she said, clasping the glass in her warm hands and sipping the amber liquid through tinkling ice cubes. 'Delicious! I didn't realise I was so thirsty.'

He sat down with his glass of beer and stretched out his long legs. He looked very relaxed for once. His manner with her so far had been guarded and yet not unfriendly. Perhaps Miles was wrong. She was tempted to relax a little.

She said casually, 'I saw that television programme on Kendall's Kingdom.'

He snorted. 'Huh! Typical sort of propaganda. Why they always have to glamorise and over-dramatise perfectly ordinary everyday happenings ...' He broke off, disgust in his tone.

'You didn't care for it?'

'No. If I'd known they were going to dress

it up like that I might have had second thoughts about letting them do it. I was led to believe that it would just be a straight-forward documentary. Kendall's Kingdom!' He laughed to himself mockingly.

'It's big enough to be a kingdom,' she said.

'And I the king?' he murmured with a sly glance, referring to her jibe.

Karen blushed. 'Well, perhaps president would be more appropriate,' she offered with half a smile. 'You're more actively involved than a king would be, in this day and age anyway.'

He chuckled. 'I wonder you don't also liken me to a business tycoon. That's been done before, of course, and I don't care much for that image either.'

'I wouldn't have thought running a hospital was quite like a business,' she said naïvely.

'It is,' he assured her. 'It's no good being efficient in the wards and sloppy in the books. There was a terrible amount of waste through inefficiency when I first came here. Nobody kept proper account of anything. The returns and reports were largely fiction invented to fit the existing chaos.'

This, Karen reflected suddenly, was the most human she had seen him and the first time he had talked to her in this way without sparring. Perhaps he was not such an ogre after all and perhaps he was not plotting some dire revenge. Miles had been watching too many television hospital serials, she decided, amused, and she must remember to chide him about it.

They chatted on about the hospital, the town, and were just getting to more personal subjects when someone came out on to the verandah to call everyone in for the speeches and a presentation to Alex. Guy, of course, was required for that. Karen was not sure whether she felt disappointed because this new rapport had been broken or relieved that personal issues had been avoided.

Once back in the main room, Guy disappeared and Karen looked for Miles, whom she found looking for her.

'Where have you been?' he asked, slipping an arm proprietorially around her waist.

'I was outside talking to Dr. Kendall.'

His eyes narrowed suspiciously. 'Were you indeed!'

'I could hardly refuse to talk to him,' she answered rather sharply, 'and it was very hot in here.'

Miles gave her a look which for some reason infuriated her.

The next morning Karen drove Alex to the

airfield as Miles had been called out to attend an urgent case in the town and had asked her to do it.

'He can give you any last-minute tips he thinks of,' Miles said, and Karen was grateful for the opportunity to go over one or two points with Alex.

'I don't think you'll make it into the air with that load,' she said laughingly as she saw the pile of suitcases, parcels and boxes that Alex was taking with him.

Alex just grinned. 'She'll be right!'

Karen felt a little sad saying goodbye to Alex because he had been very friendly and helpful and she knew she would miss him, as Miles would, too. The two men had been working together for over two years. Alex hugged her warmly and wished her good luck.

'Don't let Guy get you down,' he said with a smile. 'He's okay really.'

'I'm sure,' she murmured non-committally. Last night she had even begun to think so. 'Goodbye, Alex. All the best for a very happy future.'

He pressed her hand. 'Thanks. Take good care of the *Jabiru*, won't you, Karen. I'm rather fond of her!'

'Come back and see her some time!' Karen called after his departing figure.

She started to wave his plane off and then walked slowly over to the car park. She was just about to get into Miles' car to return to the hospital when another car hurtled into the car park, kicking up a cloud of dust as the driver braked sharply. It was Dr. Kendall. He saw Karen at once.

'Emergency!' he barked at her. 'We've got to go right away.'

'Where?'

'The mining camp out East. Don't stand around wasting time, girl!' He grabbed her arm and pulled her along after him. 'It's a matter of life and death!'

Karen's stomach fluttered apprehensively. Alex had gone. This was her first emergency flight and she was alone. A matter of life and death.

CHAPTER SEVEN

While Karen prepared hastily for take-off, Guy told her a few sketchy details about the accident. Apparently a heavy piece of equipment being delivered to the mine site had rolled out of control while being unloaded and had turned over the truck that had brought it, pinning one of the men by his legs.

'How dreadful!' she breathed in horror. 'And he's got to wait until we get there ...' Suddenly the delay seemed interminable.

'They've got a first-aid kit, of course,' said Guy. 'They'll give him a shot of morphine if the pain is too bad. Meanwhile they're rigging up a crane to lift the truck off him.' He ran his fingers through his hair impatiently and said, 'You know what shock can do?' more to himself than to her.

Briefly it registered with Karen that this was the first time she had seen Guy Kendall's cool even marginally disturbed, not counting the time he was airsick. It was not panic disturbing him now but simply the urgent need to reach the injured man.

Karen knew, too, what a reassuring affect their arrival would have on the people involved in the accident, not only the victim but those trying to help him. There was partial relief in being airborne, but for all of the several hundred kilometres they had to travel she could feel Guy mentally trying to push the aircraft through the sky at a speed faster than it was capable of. He did not say much during the flight.

The strip where Karen had to put the plane down was more rugged than she had expected. It was a mining camp they had not visited before and Karen did not see the potholes until it was too late. Fortunately none was deep enough to cause damage to the aircraft and the worst that happened was that she slewed off at an angle near the end of the run in.

She waited for Guy to comment, expecting a curled lip and a caustic comment, but all he said was, 'About time they did some work on this strip. Looks like the moon surface with all those potholes. I bet it hasn't been graded since the wet. Come on.'

Karen allowed herself a brief moment of uplifted spirits. His remarks were as good as if he had said he did not consider the bumpy landing her fault. She climbed down after him.

Greetings from the men who met them were perfunctory and they scarcely gave Karen a glance. A man's life was at stake and for once they were not interested in pretty faces.

One man said, 'Smart work, Doc, getting here so quickly. We didn't expect you yet.'

'Thank the pilot,' he answered abruptly. The man turned and grinned at Karen briefly and gratefully.

She set about her usual practice of pegging the plane down so that any sudden gust of wind could not capsize it, but Guy barked impatiently at her, 'Leave that! Let the men do it. I need you with me.' He grasped her arm and ran with her to a Land-Rover which was waiting with its engines running.

Karen did not argue. Hands as competent as hers would secure the aircraft, she felt certain. It was a tense hot journey to the mining camp, fortunately only a short distance away. Karen's later recollection was a vague notion of shimmering buildings, the sharp dark blue shadows of mid-afternoon and the silence.

As she alighted from the truck she heard someone say, 'We're having a job moving it, Doc. We might have to cut him free. We waited for you ...'

Guy took one look at the situation and answered grimly, 'So long as *I* don't have to cut him free,' Karen shuddered, knowing that he was afraid that an on-the-spot amputation might be necessary.

The man who was injured was shaded from the blazing sun by a makeshift canopy and had been made as comfortable as possible by his mates who now stood around in silent, fidgety groups, their faces grim and anxious until they saw the doctor, and then the rugged sunburnt features seemed to relax a little. Karen glimpsed a bloodstained pad on the injured man's leg where evidently there was a bad gash. There was a dark stain on the ground below the bandage. He had refused all sedatives until the doctor arrived and although he had lost a lot of blood he was still conscious. A deathly pallor showed through his tan and pain clouded the flickering eyes. Nevertheless, at the sight of them, he managed to smile and actually winked at Karen.

'Gee, Doc, am I in heaven already?' he asked in a slow, rasping voice. 'Who's the angel?'

'Don't be so optimistic, Tom,' said Guy, kneeling beside him. It was obvious that they were well known to each other. 'I reckon you're more likely bound for the other place, but not this time, mate.'

A chuckle escaped the man's lips. 'I thought I was a goner, Doc, you bet your life I did.

Boy, when she started to roll, there was no holding her ...' He glanced at Karen again, 'Well, if you're not an angel then I reckon I might change me mind and stick around a bit longer. Things seem to have improved!'

'Cut the chat, Tom,' said Guy firmly. 'You're going to need all your strength shortly. You've lost a fair bit of blood so first of all we're going to fix you up with a drip. Same as giving a donation, only this time you'll be on the receiving end.'

'Sounds fair,' said the man with a weak grin. 'I've given mine often enough. 'Bout time I got some back.'

Guy glanced at Karen and she nodded briefly and leapt to carry out the necessary operation. She saw Guy wriggling under the precariously balanced truck and load to get a closer look at Tom's legs and to assess his injuries as far as he could. He managed to apply a more effective bandage to the nasty gash on Tom's thigh, a difficult task in the confined space. Karen felt the tension in the men standing around mount again as they waited for his verdict. The most relaxed amongst them, she thought, was ironically the injured man, although that was probably due more to shock than self-control. Nevertheless, he was a very brave young man.

Someone clapped a wide-brimmed hat on Karen's head and she felt instant relief from the scorching sun. She smiled down at the injured man. Suddenly he reached out his hand and clasped her free one, holding it tightly, betraying in his fingers the fear that was not in his face.

'I think I'd rather die than lose me legs, Nurse,' he whispered.

'Neither's happened yet, Tom,' she soothed softly, 'so don't go crossing bridges.'

His eyes met hers, looking for the truth. He was about twenty-five or six, she guessed, a good-looking young man with brawny arms and broad shoulders and with a day's beard growth on his chin.

'What's your name, Nurse?' he asked.

'Karen Lalor.'

'You're pretty.'

'You're not bad-looking yourself!'

'Is it Nurse Lalor?'

'Sister, actually.'

'Triple certificated?' He grinned at her cheekily now although his grasp of her fingers was still tight and she nodded. He said, 'My sister's a nurse, back in Sydney.'

'Don't try to talk,' she said, 'you know what the doctor said.'

'I wish he'd hurry up.'

As he spoke Guy eased himself out and knelt beside the injured man.

'Sorry to keep you hanging around like this, Tom,' he said gently, 'but you've landed yourself in a tricky spot. We've got to work something out.'

'Give us the worst news first, Doc,' demanded Tom, gritting his teeth. 'Do I lose me legs?'

Karen waited for Guy to tell a non-committal but comforting white lie but it was soon clear that he knew his patient too well to do that.

'I can't tell yet, Tom,' he said bluntly. 'I'll bet you two to one against, though. We'll have a better idea once we get you free of the truck, but we can't be quite certain until we get you back to the hospital.' He paused, eyeing the man speculatively. 'You don't have to put up with all this, Tom. I can knock you out if you like.'

Tom shook his head, clearly more terrified of not being conscious than of enduring pain. 'No thanks. I'll keep an eye on the nurse for you, Doc, and then I won't feel a thing!'

'Okay.' Guy exchanged a glance with Karen. 'I'll give him a local.' He smiled faintly. 'Don't let him get too fresh, Sister!'

'No, Doctor,' she answered, deadpan, but

141

felt sure she caught a twinkle in his eyes. A wave of relief washed over her. Surely this dash of humour could only mean that Guy was confident that everything would be all right.

He said, 'Tell Tom a story to keep his mind off what we're doing.' When Karen looked taken aback he added sharply, 'Just talk to him, Sister. You know how to do that, don't you?'

She gulped and nodded. She did know, but she had never had to do it in circumstances like these. She could not think of a thing to say to Tom. The injured man looked up at her curiously. 'Tell me all about yourself, Karen, that's what I'd like to hear. Go on, I'm all ears.'

She hesitated. She did not want to talk about herself but she could think of nothing else.

'Are you married?' Tom asked.

'No ... I was engaged ... once ...' she began falteringly, and then without really meaning to she found herself unburdening to this unknown man the story of Sean. She told him everything, of the happiness, of the anxiety when Sean was ill, of her grief. That it was scarcely the sort of story to cheer a man up, occurred to her more than once but Tom's eyes were fixed on her face full of interest and there seemed no way she could stop now she had started.

The crucial time while they lifted the truck should have seemed interminable; the lifting operation was necessarily slow and laborious as everything depended on freeing Tom Jarvis without injuring him further in the process; but Karen scarcely noticed the minutes ticking by or the whirr of machinery, the clanking of straining metal, or even the stiffness in her limbs from the awkward position she was in holding the intravenous blood drip connected to Tom's arm.

Once she wondered in dismay what Guy might say afterwards about her choice of story, but whenever she attempted to change the subject, Tom squeezed her hand and said, 'Go on ...'

Suddenly a change came over his face. He broke into her narrative and smiled broadly. 'They've done it!' He breathed thankfully. 'They've got it off!'

His legs must have been quite numb, Karen knew, from the local anaesthetic, but nevertheless he had known when the crushing weight was lifted from them. She glanced over her shoulder at Guy. He held up a thumb and gave her a brief smile.

'Not long now, Tom,' he said. 'We've just got to get you out from underneath, that's all. Grit your teeth.'

Karen saw that the most dangerous part was yet to be achieved. Guy and another man now had to drag Tom out from under the poised truck. One false move ... As she saw Guy's head close beneath the tons of metal suddenly her heart lurched into her throat. He could so easily be crushed, too ... That she, too, was in some danger, did not occur to her.

'We're going to swing him round,' came Guy's taut voice. 'Hold steady, Karen.' The steel ropes holding the precariously balanced truck and its runaway load creaked ominously.

Karen tensed and involuntarily closed her eyes for a second. When she opened them there was a sickening crunch of metal that sent a wave of nausea flowing through her but then she saw Guy and his voice, triumphant, was like a douche of cool refreshing water.

'Okay, all clear now, Tom. No worries. Relax.' He smiled at Karen. 'We all can.'

Karen looked down at the patient. She was momentarily shocked to see that his eyes were closed and the hand that had held hers was limply beside him. Suppressing a bubble of panic she pressed her fingers against his wrist, feeling for his pulse. Relief flooded through her once more as it fluttered to her touch. Tom Jarvis had understandably just fainted.

Little was said now. There were a few

murmurs of relief but everyone knew that the final verdict would come later when the injured man had been taken back to the hospital. Someone thrust a mug of tea into Karen's free hand and she took a few sips. It was very sweet and very refreshing in spite of the heat.

She passed the mug back to the hand that had offered it and then as soon as they were ready walked beside the stretcher on to which Tom had been lifted, still holding her bottle aloft. The slow drive to the airstrip was the worst part of what followed. Guy was insistent that Tom was not jolted about too much. To Karen he confided that he suspected a spinal injury as well but he could not be sure yet.

The airstrip was unexpectedly a hive of activity. Men with shovels were bashing earth into the potholes, endeavouring to improve the ground for take-off. A grader, it seemed, had been unobtainable to do the job properly, which in this remote area was scarcely surprising. Karen surveyed the scene with a few misgivings but there was no time to fuss. She had landed safely, no doubt she could take off safely, too.

On the take-off run she had a few more moments of anxiety but steeled her concentration to the task of becoming airborne without incident. Tom Jarvis's life depended on her at that moment—all their lives did, she thought.

Guy probably did not hear her heartfelt exclamation, 'We made it!' as the tiny plane soared into the air. He was too busy looking after the patient in the rear of plane. Karen waved once to the figures clustered around the truck at the end of the airstrip as she banked, and a few moments later they were no more than mere specks on the red dust, specks with long, distorted shadows. The sun was almost at the horizon.

Karen was due to go off duty when they arrived back at the hospital. There were others ready and waiting to take over from her. The theatre had been prepared for the emergency and all Karen had to do was watch the stretcher carried in once she had been relieved.

She could not, however, bring herself to go home. She had to stay until Guy had operated. She had to know whether Tom would lose his legs or not. She had come close to him in those tense moments at the mining camp, she realised, and in some strange way she owed him something, a debt he would never be aware of.

It was a long time before she saw Guy leave the theatre and walk wearily along to his office.

Tentatively she followed him, tapping lightly on his door, hoping he would understand her anxiety and not think it an intrusion.

'Come in!' The voice was weary, a little impatient. She pushed open the door.

'Dr. Kendall ... I just wondered ... how is he?'

'Karen!' He was startled to see her. 'I thought you'd have gone home hours ago. You must be dead on your feet.'

'No. I mean ... I had to wait, to know how Tom is.'

His eyes held hers, a smile, faintly mocking, tilted the corners of his mouth, stretching the lines of tiredness and tension. The light from the desk lamp cast deep shadows across his face, carving it up into jagged planes, giving him a gaunt expression.

'Did you fall for him, then?' he asked sardonically. 'He evidently fell quite heavily for you.'

Karen flinched. 'That is a remark in rather poor taste,' she stated icily. She was disappointed. If there had been any rapport between them today it must have been purely professional. He was showing that his contempt for her was unchanged.

'Well, you held his hand and told him your life-story.'

'Only because he asked ... and you said ...'

He interrupted her. 'Sit down, Karen. I wanted to talk to you anyway.'

She sat nervously on the edge of the chair. Was he going to reprimand her for talking about herself to the patient and especially about dwelling on the morbid part of her life unnecessarily? She wished she had not done it but it was too late for regrets now.

'Tom is luckier than he should be,' Guy said, facing her again, his hands on the desk, leaning slightly forward towards her, the angle of the light accentuating his tiredness even more now until she felt a sudden unexpected wave of sympathy for him and a foolish desire to smooth his brow with caressing fingers. A pause as he slumped into his chair. 'No serious internal injuries and only one leg is fractured badly in three places. The other has a pretty straightforward fracture of the fibula and there's that nasty gash. It needed considerable stitching. It may need a graft.'

'Sounds serious enough,' she said, 'but I'm glad he won't have to lose his legs.'

'No way!' Unexpectedly he smiled and instantly the look of tiredness vanished. 'Things often look worse than they are.'

She smiled back, warmed suddenly. 'Yes, that's true. Tom was expecting the worst.'

148

'Well, in that case he'll have a pleasant surprise when he wakes.' He regarded her intently for a moment, then said, 'You probably did him a lot of good telling him the story of your life. Sympathy for another person is always ...'

'I didn't do it because I wanted sympathy!' She was appalled at his suggestion.

'I'm sure you didn't. I can see you wish you hadn't, but you couldn't think of anything else to talk about. The situation shocked you, too, didn't it? You haven't been on the scene of an accident like that before?'

'No, as a matter of fact I haven't.' She looked down at her hands tightly clasped in her lap, sure he was going to find some fault with her performance today.

'I thought not. You handled it very well, Karen.'

She was startled, and gulped, 'Thank you.' Her heart was beating rapidly all of a sudden, which was quite ridiculous, just because he had said a word of praise.

'As a matter of fact the experience probably did you a lot of good,' Guy continued, 'in more ways than one.'

She nodded. It was true. Talking to Tom had been the last stage of what had started weeks ago, what Miles had unwittingly helped along, and which today was finally completed.

Her heart had finally been emptied of its misery.

Guy Kendall stood up. He glanced at his watch. 'You must be hungry. I know I'm starving. Can you keep awake long enough for a bite to eat?'

'It really doesn't matter, Dr. Kendall ...' she began, intending to refuse his offer because although her feelings towards him had been tempered during the last few minutes and in contrast to the first minute after entering his office she now almost liked him, she felt nervous of being alone with him.

'Guy's the name,' he corrected, smiling. 'Do, for heaven's sake, stop that formal Dr. Kendall business except in the wards. I call you Karen, don't I?'

'Sometimes,' she murmured.

'Well, come along, we're going to have a meal. Doctor's orders!'

Karen took a few minutes to splash her face with cold water and comb her hair which had been flattened under a scarf all day. They left the hospital in Guy's car and drove to the Wirrumburra Hotel. It was late but the hotel was willing to provide a meal. Dr. Guy Kendall had no difficulty in getting what he wanted, that was obvious. The dining room was deserted except for them.

'Professionaly speaking, how did you enjoy your first emergency?' Guy asked casually as they waited for the main course to be served. He sipped a glass of beer, looking intently at her over the rim of the glass, weighing her up in a most disconcerting way.

'Even speaking professionally, does one ever enjoy emergencies?' she countered.

'You coped.'

Almost a second compliment! She said, 'As you said before, it was a bit of a shock. I've never assisted in circumstances like that before. I learnt a lot.'

'You probably will learn a lot of things here that a city hospital can't teach you,' he told her, wryly.

'The trouble is I won't have much chance, will I?' she remarked, seizing the opportunity. 'You'll have a new pilot soon.'

'And you won't stay as a nurse?'

'No!' She was still definite about that.

He twisted the half-empty glass in his hands. Karen took a sip of her chilled white wine. Guy said, 'You had a taste of how tough it can be today. It takes stamina. We could get an emergency like that several times in a row. You'd have to turn out every time.'

'I gather Nurse Maguire and Nurse Morwell and others always manage to cope,' Karen

151

pointed out.

'They don't fly the aircraft as well.'

'Well, we could always take another nurse along as back-up,' Karen argued.

He laughed softly. 'I don't think you'd really like that, would you?'

He was right of course. She wanted to be a pilot-nurse, not just a nurse, not just a pilot. It incensed her that he considered the combination too tough for a woman. She was certain she would always be able to cope even if they had ten emergencies in a row.

'I'm a lot tougher than you think,' she said hotly. 'Just because I'm only five foot three and eight stone doesn't mean ...'

'And thirty-four, twenty-two, thirty-four ...' he put in with a mocking grin.

She pulled her lips together. 'Your measurements are not quite accurate, Doctor!' she retorted but did not correct his minor mistake in her vital statistics. 'And isn't it time you started thinking in metrics?'

He laughed, his eyes narrowed. 'You have a fiery temper, Karen, my dear, but do please remember to call me Guy when we're off duty even if you are angry.'

'I am not angry!'

'No? Very defensive, though.'

'And why not? You seem to have a pretty

poor view of women. You don't seem to think—even when there's evidence to the contrary—that we are good for anything much.'

He inclined his head and said sardonically, 'Oh, you're quite wrong. Women are very good indeed for some things.'

The innuendo brought a quick flush of colour to Karen's cheeks, much to her chagrin.

'That's about the level of remark I would expect from you!' she hissed at him.

'I was thinking particularly of nursing,' he countered blandly.

He was teasing her now, goading her. All her kinder feelings towards him evaporated once more as she seethed, wondering why he had bothered to bring her here for a meal, pretending concern, when all he could do was bicker with her.

'I know you don't like me,' she said quietly, keeping her anger under control, 'but can't we just do our jobs and forget our differences of opinion? I should like to change the subject.'

His eyebrows rose in hurt surprise. 'You mislead yourself, Karen. I like you very much. I'm afraid it is you who do not like me. Perhaps ...' he paused again eyeing her speculatively, 'perhaps I shall have to do more to change that.'

Somehow he always managed to leave her bereft of a suitable answer. Their meal arrived before she could frame a retort to his last remark, and when the waiter had departed he lifted his knife and fork and glancing across at Karen, said, unexpectedly:

'Do you play tennis?'

'Yes.'

'Good. Then we will pit our skills on the court at the weekend. If your serve is as fiery as your temper it should be a stimulating game.'

'You're mocking me again,' she accused.

'My dear Karen, I'm only trying to be friendly.'

Was he? Karen could not be sure. One minute she felt that he did like her and she liked him but the next they were sparring again. It was very exhausting. She applied herself to her meal and for some minutes there was silence at the table.

When coffee was served they went into the lounge, also almost deserted now. Guy ordered liqueurs and they settled back in comfortable easy chairs. Karen felt relaxed after the meal but she was still wary of Guy. He was so unpredictable. He lit a pipe and puffed contentedly at it. He looks just like any ordinary family man, she thought, watching him, and yet he has the reputation of a philanderer.

'You haven't always lived up here, have you?' she asked, as the silence extended and became uncomfortable.

He looked sharply at her. 'I was born here,' he said, 'but I had to go away to study, naturally. I stayed away rather longer than I should have done. It paid off in the long run in experience, of course, but there are ... other things ...' He broke off, staring into the distance beyond her, lost momentarily in some private thought.

'It must be quite a responsibility being a doctor as well as running a sheep station,' she said.

'Two. My uncle's as well as my father's. They both died within months of each other and my uncle had no children of his own, so everything came to me.'

'Your mother?' Karen asked, since he did not seem to mind these personal questions and she was curious about him in spite of herself. 'Does she live up here or in Perth?' She had not been in evidence at Wirrumburra Downs and Karen had wondered about her then.

His face clouded. 'My mother ... I'm afraid she's dead, too.'

'Oh ... I'm sorry.' Karen wished she had not probed. It was obviously very painful.

He did not speak again for a moment or two,

then said, 'It must seem very remote up here after living in the city all your life.'

'Not all my life. I was born on a farm. I like the wide open spaces, especially from the air. The country up here has a grandeur I had not expected. I've never been as far north as this before. I hadn't realised the colours were so vivid. I mean, I knew all about red dust and iron hills and all that, and I've seen plenty of pictures, but the reality is so different ... it's something you feel as much as see ...' She stopped, aware that she was rambling on incoherently, trying to put into words what she had previously not even rationalised. She felt embarrassed but he did not seem to notice.

'It either claims you or repels you,' he said thoughtfully. 'Be careful, though, that yours are not just romantic notions. It's a harsh land but it does have its own beauty for those who have eyes to see.' He looked at her with sudden eagerness. 'If you really like it that much, I'll show you some things you'll never see properly from the air, one day when we've got time. There's a gorge at Wirrumburra Downs, not far from the homestead, a deep shadowy canyon with a waterfall, rock faces that look as though someone painted horizontal stripes on them, ghost gums, caves, an astonishing oasis.'

'I'd love to see it,' she said.

'We'll take a day off sometime,' he said, and she wondered if he really meant it. The prospect half thrilled her, half disconcerted her. It was such an about-face on his part to make such a friendly suggestion. Or was she wrong about him after all?

He drove her home later and walked up to the front porch at Ma Carson's place with her. He rested his arm languidly across her shoulders as they strolled up the front path, turning her to face him as they stopped on the porch. His face was barely discernible in the gloom.

'Make sure you get a good sleep,' he said, sounding genuinely concerned. 'It won't matter if you're late tomorrow. I'll warn Matron.'

'I don't need a lot of sleep,' she said. 'I'll be fine in the morning.'

His eyes were dark, unfathomable in the dim light, his mouth quirky.

'Tough little customer, aren't you? But you don't have to keep proving it, Karen.'

'I'm not!'

He touched her chin with an admonitory finger. 'Now, now, no fireworks. We don't want to wake Ma Carson, do we?' Very gently he tilted her chin up and bent his head, his lips touching hers with a soft warmth that sent a shiver running down her spine. He moved his mouth on hers in a tentative exploratory way, with scarcely any pressure and yet with such a tantalising touch she was hypnotised and made no effort to draw away although not even a restraining arm prevented her. Momentarily, her temples throbbed and she felt a wild desire to fling herself into his arms, to seek the fulfilment that his kiss promised, but before she could give in to this impulse he had lifted his mouth and drawn back from her.

He smiled down at her and gave her arm a swift, almost fatherly pat.

'Off you go! You do need some rest whatever you say. Goodnight, Karen.'

'Goodnight, Guy,' she whispered and watched him get into his car and drive off, while she stood transfixed to the spot. Her lips still burned although he had scarcely touched them and her whole body shook with suppressed emotion.

As she watched the winking red lights of his car vanish around the corner of the street she knew without doubt that Dr. Guy Kendall was even more dangerously attractive than she had first thought. She knew, too, that she must be on her guard against him. Because of Sean she had starved herself of love for too long, but now she was free and, as Guy had just proved to her, vulnerable.

She must be very careful, she told herself, as she went slowly and thoughtfully to her room, not to let her emotions betray her again as they so nearly had tonight. It was a danger made all the more dangerous by the fact that she had suddenly begun to like Guy.

CHAPTER EIGHT

If Karen had ever entertained even vaguely any idea that Wirrumburra was a sleepy sort of town and that combining flying with nursing would mean a ninety per cent emphasis on nursing, she soon found out how wrong she was. Almost as though to prove Guy's point the week that followed was a hectic one.

Scarcely was the shock and strain of the mining camp accident over than Karen was required to fly Guy out to a remote station to bring in a patient suffering from appendicitis. There was a woman having a baby and suffering from an ante-partum haemorrhage, then another man with severe abdominal pains that did not respond to the treatment prescribed over the radio, a child with meningitis, and all had to be brought in to Wirrumburra Hospital in the *Jabiru*. Karen thought ruefully once or twice that if she needed any practice in landing and taking off she was certainly getting it.

Always in the back of her mind, however,

was the knowledge that her job was only temporary. The more she became absorbed in it the more she reminded herself of this fact. After the night they had dined together and he had kissed her there was no noticeable change in her relationship with Guy. It continued on a see-saw course with him sometimes friendly, sometimes brusque, and she sometimes hopping mad with him, sometimes completely at ease.

When she reported to Guy on her return from one trip she was alone with him for a few minutes in his office before Miles came in. He looked her up and down with a half smile and she was acutely conscious of his smouldering eyes, the strong expressive hands with fingers linked as his chin rested on them and the fact that he emanated a very definite masculinity, a physical attraction that she told herself had nothing whatever to do with whether a person was likeable or not. She always felt uncomfortable with him because of it, and the galling part was that she suspected he was aware of it.

'I hope the pace isn't getting you down,' he said in his quiet but highly charged voice. 'You look rather strained, Karen.'

She stiffened at the implied criticism. 'I imagine anyone, even you, looks a little tired at the end of a day sometimes,' she said haughtily, trying to forget the weariness in her bones and the ache that was developing behind her eyes as a result of intense concentration and continuous glare.

His eyebrows moved in a quick up and down movement and there was a twitch of annoyance at the corner of his mouth. Karen belatedly remembered that he was her superior and that she had no right to be rude to him even if he provoked her. She met his gaze stubbornly. What did it matter if she did retort when he provoked her? Letting fly at him eased the tension fractionally.

He said, just as quietly as before, 'Do you always take kindness as criticism?'

That really got under her skin. 'No,' she replied levelly, 'not when kindness is intended.'

He shrugged and turned his attention to the report she had placed on his desk. Karen waited for him to dismiss her but he did not speak. Fortunately, Miles came in and broke the tension. While he spoke to Guy Karen found herself with a startling and unwelcome thought. Looking at the two men she suddenly thought that while Miles was nice, Guy was the kind of man you could fall in love with even in spite of yourself, and he would tear your heart to shreds leaving you more shattered than after the loss of someone as dear as Sean ...

She squashed the thought instantly. There was no way in the world she would ever fall in love with Guy Kendall! Heaven forbid! He would never tear her heart into little bits and throw them away lightly. She was not that vulnerable.

He raised his head and looked straight at her as though he had read her thoughts.

'I think Karen needs to unwind a little,' he remarked in a condescending tone. 'Perhaps you should take her out to dinner, Miles, if you're both off duty. You have better bedside manners than I.'

Miles glanced at Karen, and she said swiftly, resenting Guy's arrogance, 'Thanks for the prescription, but Miles has already invited me.'

She hoped Miles would not deny this and to her relief he did not. Later when they were seated at a table in a corner of the hotel dining room, he reminded her of it.

'Had he been needling you?'

Karen nodded. 'He always does, Miles. Sometimes I'm not sure if he means to or if I'm just prickly where he's concerned, but he twists things ... or rather invites you to twist what he says ... oh, I don't know. I can't stand the man.'

'He's not a bad bloke really,' Miles said loyally, 'when you get to know him. He just knows what he wants, that's all, and he gets it. You have to respect his judgement. He's usually right.'

'The King can do no wrong,' Karen said dismally, feeling that even Miles had deserted her.

'Don't be bitter, Karen.'

She laughed suddenly. 'Sorry! I suppose it just needles me that he's so pig-headed. I can do the job. He doesn't deny it. He can't find fault and yet he won't admit he's wrong. It's so unfair.'

'It is strenuous, though, you must admit.'

'Don't you start!' she exclaimed. 'This week was unusually hectic. I know that's true because Kelly said so. I'm not on the verge of cracking up. I can stand a bit of pressure, Miles, as well as anyone.'

'It isn't just pressure,' said Miles, 'it's the atmosphere here. After a while it gets you down unless you're born to it like Guy, like the station people—and most of them escape south from time to time. The heat, the isolation, the loneliness, it can make you want to scream eventually.'

Karen said sympathetically. 'It's got to you, Miles?'

'Starting to, I guess. I'm city bred like you, Karen. Like you I itched to get away from it, to quit the artificial rat-race, to find real people, real life, but ...'

'You go down for holidays.'

He shrugged. 'And every time it's harder to come back. I've enjoyed the experience, don't think I haven't, and working for Guy just has to be a great opportunity, but it's ... it's difficult to explain. Sooner or later you want a change.'

'You won't renew your contract then?'

'No. Lately I've felt the tug more and more.' He saw her anxiety and added, 'Don't worry, I won't be leaving before you. I've got another six months to go.'

Karen asked, 'Has Guy done anything yet about getting a pilot, do you know, Miles?'

He shook his head. 'He hasn't mentioned it to me. Obviously he won't trust me to engage one after the grave mistake I made choosing you!'

Karen smiled ruefully. 'I suppose not! You really did blot your copybook there, Miles.'

He shot her a speculative glance. 'Guy's a fool, in my opinion, but he'll have to find that out for himself.'

'He never will.'

Miles asked, 'Linda arrives this week, doesn't she?'

'Yes, she's still determined to see it through.'

'Good for her.'

Two days before Linda was due to arrive, Karen was on night duty at the hospital. So, too, was Miles. Things were quiet. There were few patients and none of them serious cases. When a light flicked on on the board Karen was surprised. She hurried along to the patient who had called her. It was old Mrs. Bardwell, who suffered recurring bouts of bronchitis and had developed pleurisy. She was almost well enough to go home.

'I can't sleep, Nurse,' she complained softly and apologetically. 'I'm sorry to bother you, dear, but I'm just lying here thinking about Lennie and what I should do ...'

Karen touched the gnarled old hand gripping the sheet. 'That won't help, will it? But I understand how you feel. It is a problem.' The old lady's nephew was in hospital in a country town several hundred kilometres away where he worked as a shearer. His wife had recently died and he was bringing up his son alone. The boy came to Mrs. Bardwell from time to time, but his father did not like to lose touch with him for long. Karen knew about

166

it from previous chats to Mrs. Bardwell.

'I'll get you a sleeping pill,' she said.

Mrs. Bardwell propped herself up on her pillows. 'No, dear, I'd rather not have one of those things. I've never had much trouble getting to sleep and I don't want to start taking drugs now. Would you mind ... do you think I could just have a cup of tea?'

Karen smiled. 'Of course, and I'll have one, too. I could do with a cup myself and I'll drink mine with you and we can have a little chat.'

The old lady smiled. 'You're a good girl.'

Karen went to the pantry and made the tea. She took Miles a cup and told him where she would be for the next little while. He promised to keep his eye on the board. When Karen returned to Mrs. Bardwell's room she found to her satisfaction that the old lady had fallen asleep.

As she walked back down the corridor again, Karen now noticed that there was a light under the door of Guy Kendall's office. Perhaps the cleaners had forgotten to switch it off. It was Guy's night off so he couldn't be there. She balanced the tray on her hip and turned the handle of the door. It fell open silently.

'Oh!' Karen was surprised to see Guy's dark head look up from the desk where he was still working. 'I didn't know you were still here.'

'I stayed to do some work on an article I'm writing,' he said, and yawned. 'Is that tea?' His face in the pool of light from the desk lamp looked pale and drawn.

'Would you like a cup?'

'I would. I was just thinking about asking someone to make one.'

Karen walked into the room and placed the tray on the desk. 'I made this for Mrs. Bardwell. She said she couldn't sleep and wouldn't take a pill but when I went back she'd dropped off.'

'Two cups?' he asked quizzically.

'I was going to have one with her and chat for a bit. She's worrying about her nephew. I thought it might help her to sleep if she just talked about it for a while.'

His face softened slightly. 'Quite probably it would have done. Pills don't solve problems.' He glanced at her. 'Well, you might as well have your tea, too. Sit down, Karen.'

She was reluctant to do so and yet in a way pleased he had asked her. His words had not been far short of a compliment—tacit approval at any rate.

There was an awkward silence after she had poured the two cups of tea, offered him sugar and then returned to her seat, balancing her cup and saucer nervously, waiting for him to speak because words had failed her.

Eventually when he still said nothing and she was aware, although she kept her eyes averted, of him looking intently at her, she ventured, 'What is your article about?'

'Aboriginal health,' he said. 'I've made some intensive studies of their particular problems over the past few years. I was talking about my ideas to one of the doctors in a research team that was up here recently and he said I ought to write something for one of the medical journals.' He smiled, modestly for him, Karen thought, and shuffled the papers. 'I'm not much good at writing but it's all in there. Trouble is it ought to be typewritten for publication. Still, I daresay if they're sufficiently interested they'll wade through it.'

His diffidence surprised Karen. She suddenly heard herself saying, 'I could type it for you if you like.'

For a moment he looked surprised. Then he said drily, 'Ah, yes, I remember. You gave up nursing to become a secretary, didn't you?'

She countered with, 'And I gave that up to go back to nursing.'

He shuffled the papers together. 'I'd be very grateful if you would type it for me, Karen, but you surely have other things to do with your free time?'

There was too much emphasis on the 'other' and she knew he was referring to Miles. As she had no intention of correcting him, she said, 'I surely may choose how I spend my spare time. If you prefer not to ...'

'Karen!' His exclamation cut across her words, and she swallowed hard at his thunderous look. She had gone too far again, provoking him now. Oh, it really was an impossible situation. They couldn't have a normal conversation without striking sparks off each other.

As he drew in a deep breath she did not wait for him to upbraid her but said quickly, 'I only meant ...'

Suddenly he was laughing. 'Good heavens, girl, I don't think you do know what you mean half the time. You're as prickly as a cactus. Anyone would think I aimed to eat you alive!'

Karen cringed. He was mocking her now, his dark penetrating eyes ripping the mask off her face and probing into her mind.

'I'm sorry,' she muttered, angry that she had let herself be beaten by him, wishing she had never offered to type his manuscript, wishing she had never agreed to stay, wishing ...

He was saying calmly, 'As I said, I would be very grateful if you would type the article for me, Karen. I've just got a few more

170

sentences to add and then I'll let you have it. You can use the office typewriter.'

'It won't take long,' she said. 'I'll do it tomorrow either before or after I go on duty.'

'Thank you,' he said again, and as his pencil began to tap very lightly and measured on the blotter, Karen jumped up to let him get on with it. She picked up the cups and put them back on the tray. Her hands shook a little as she retrieved his from practically under his nose and when he glanced up at her with a look that was hard to evaluate, the cup wobbled on the saucer. She placed it hastily on the tray and beat a retreat.

She did not go straight back to the pantry with the tray but retraced her steps to Mrs. Bardwell's room to see if the old lady was still asleep. She was breathing heavily but was sound asleep. Karen hoped she would not wake later and not be able to get back to sleep again but be afraid to ring her bell. Karen knew the agonies of insomnia. She had suffered from them herself for many months while Sean was ill and after his death.

She trod on silent feet along to the small pantry where she had prepared the tea. As she passed the room where Miles was, she pushed the door open and said softly, 'Won't be a minute, I'll just wash the cups.'

171

He gave her his. 'All quiet on the Wirrum-burra front,' he said with a grin.

Karen balanced the tray on her hip as she felt for the light switch in the pantry. It flicked down but the light did not come on.

'Damn!' she exclaimed softly. The bulb must have gone. She fumbled in the dark, putting the tray down on the bench by the sink, and then turned round to go out to the store cupboard along the corridor to find a new bulb Miles would put it in for her. He was tall enough to reach the socket without standing on a chair.

As she turned swiftly from the sink she saw a figure silhouetted in the doorway against the corridor light, and before she could break her plunge he had stepped forward and she had walked right into his arms. She heard him give a sharp grunt at the impact and then she felt arms tightly encircling her, heard the sound of something rustling to the floor, and someone's full sensuous lips were hot and heavy on hers.

'Miles ...' she protested in shocked amazement, trying to drag her mouth away but even as she said his name she knew it was not Miles who held her, and who stifled her protest with his mouth, pushing her head back, dragging her body hard against him as though he would

mould her to him and stamp an impression
of himself upon her. Even through the stiff
cotton of her uniform she could feel the
warmth of him, the hard pressure of his
muscular thighs against hers. The way his
mouth moved on hers brooked no resistance
and she found to her utter dismay that she
possessed none. Her lips seemed to move with
a will of their own and she knew for sure now
that what she had been suffering this past year
was not all grief, but hunger, an aching hunger
for love, love of the fierce passionate consum-
ing kind that no one she had met since Sean,
not even Miles, had aroused in her.

Karen knew that unless she found the
strength to resist Guy quickly, she would have
no resistance left at all. She fought as though
trying not to succumb to an anaesthetic, but
it was not so much Guy's strength that prevented it as her own weakness.

When he finally let her go he made it all
ten times worse by brushing his lips tenderly
against her ear and stroking the side of her
face. He whispered, 'I suppose Miles thinks
you're nice to kiss, too, Karen.' Then as she
stiffened, he added archly, 'I'm sorry if I disappointed you.'

'Miles is next door,' she whispered hoarsely,
ashamed of her reaction to him.

'So I noticed,' he said calmly. 'He told me where you were but he didn't say you were waiting in the dark!'

She said shakily, 'The bulb's gone, I was just going to get a new one. I thought ... you were Miles.'

He ran his fingers lightly down her arm. 'Not all the time, Karen, not all the time,' he mocked. He turned away saying, 'I'll fetch the bulb for you.'

He went out and Karen stood transfixed for a moment. Then she noticed dimly the scattered papers on the floor. He had dropped them when he came in. She bent down to gather them together and a moment later he was back, untwisting the old bulb and replacing it with the new one. When light flooded the little room, seeming twice as bright as it had ever seemed before, she was carefully putting the pages in numerical order.

'Karen,' he said softly, 'are you angry with me?' His hand rested lightly on her shoulder. She shrugged it off angrily.

'Yes!'

His chuckle echoed mockingly around the room. 'Good! It would have been quite uncharacteristic of you to be otherwise.' He paused for a moment, then said casually, 'I hope you don't have too much difficulty reading my handwriting, and ... by the way ... I do not approve of staff romances on duty. If you and Miles want to conduct an affair please do it in your own time and don't make assignations in darkened pantries.'

She gaped at him, utterly bereft of any response. The arrogance of the man, when *he* had kissed her! And so passionately!

She began to frame a retort but he had already turned and left the room. Karen hid her face behind the manuscript and closed her eyes. She must not ... definitely must not let the man's strong physical attraction blind her to his hatefulness.

CHAPTER NINE

Karen went alone to meet Linda. Guy, in a mood of generosity, had told her to take the whole day off in order to welcome her friend and settle her in at Ma Carson's and show her around the hospital and town. It went without saying, of course, that she was still on call to fly him anywhere he might be needed in an emergency.

'I should like you to bring Linda over to my place for a get-together tomorrow evening,' he told her as she was going off duty the night before. 'It will be a chance for her to meet her new colleagues in an informal way.'

He had left it to Kelly to arrange the get-together for her, Karen reflected ruefully, but then her introduction to Wirrumburra life had been somewhat off-beat to say the least. She said:

'Some of us will be on duty.'

'Naturally, but as my house is scarcely more than the length of a hospital corridor away I think we can arrange a relay for an hour or so each without disrupting routine too seriously. Matron is good at organising such occasions. It's been done before.' His tone was crisp, businesslike and suggested that he had no intention of unbending towards her despite a kiss. That gave her no advantage or any special position, was the clear message. Not that she wanted it to, quite the opposite, but she wished he had never kissed her at all. The memory of both occasions was still disturbing.

As she drove out to the airfield, using Miles' car, Karen kept seeing Guy's dark mocking eyes, impenetrable steely grey and yet capable of causing unwanted turmoil in her as one minute they crushed her with a withering look, the next electrified her with sensual intensity, and then caught her off guard with a rare softness or even a humorous twinkle that seemed so out of character with the rest of the time and stirred an involuntary liking for him.

She could not forget that night when they had dined together at the Wirrumburra Hotel and had talked about the country and his love of it and he had seemed pleased because she felt strongly about it, too. He had offered that night to show her the gorge near his home and had seemed to soften towards her in spite of the early fireworks. His kiss that night had been gentle, yet just as arousing as the passionate embrace of two nights ago.

He had shown no sign at first of even recalling the incident in the pantry when she had next day delivered to him the neatly typewritten pages of his manuscript. He had glanced through it and then looked up, smiling.

'Excellent. Thank you very much, Karen. It was generous of you to use some of your free time doing this for me. I'm grateful. I'll have to take you out to dinner again sometime to repay you.'

This was more fulsome thanks than she had expected, but then Guy was always surprising her. She had never met a man so unpredictable. If only he would praise her work as a nurse-pilot in similar terms and acknowledge that she could do the job by making her permanent, but she knew he never would.

'I don't expect to be repaid, it didn't take long,' she muttered, aware that her cheeks burned quite unnecessarily. She commented hesitantly, 'I thought it was a very good article.' This was true. She had been impressed by his precise, succinct dealing with the subject and his clear, factual prose. No frills, no fuss, no inconclusive speculation, just plain facts and logical conclusions set out in as orderly a fashion as an instrument tray. Still, what else ought she to have expected from such a man?

He inclined his head. 'Thank you.'

Karen instantly felt she had said the wrong thing, that he thought her presumptuous to comment. After all she knew little of the subject. She met his eyes waveringly and a desperate desire for him to fold his arms around her as he had last night washed over her.

'I must be going,' she mumbled, dragging her eyes away, turning right away from him, afraid he had seen her blatant need.

If he gave no sign of it, not even a mocking glance. He walked to the door, reaching it as he did. His hand dropped on to her shoulder.

'May I call on your generosity some other time, Karen, if the need arises? You understand the terminology better than the girls in the office.'

'Yes ... yes, of course,' she muttered.

His hand moved briefly to slide around the back of her neck in a light caress. She jumped involuntarily and there was a knock at the door. Guy's hand dropped to his side and not daring to look at him she hurried out, past the caller, murmuring, 'Hello, Miles.'

She hardly dared to look at him either and wished fervently it had not been he who wished to see Guy. Would he observe her confusion and guess the reason for it? As he had appeared to have suspected nothing of what had happened in the pantry last night she trusted he would notice nothing amiss now.

There had been tenderness in Guy's touch, Karen reflected now, just like that night after the mining camp accident. Or was she imagining it?

What did it matter anyhow? She did not want tenderness or anything else from him. She wished suddenly that he would leave her alone, find another pilot quickly and send her away. But the thought brought an odd ache. She did not want to go.

Determinedly, she switched her thoughts to Linda as she approached the airfield. She hoped she was enjoying the trip. It was a beautiful day for flying. Snowy white clouds flecked a brilliant blue sky and there was very little haze on the ground, so visibility was almost perfect to a far horizon. Glancing around her Karen wondered what Linda was thinking as she looked down on this harsh red-brown country with its ancient rugged hills, worn down and queerly shaped by eons of weather and earth movements, its scrubby trees and spinifex. She recalled again Guy's description of its hidden beauties, the river that ran through a high-cliffed gorge where ghost gums strained upwards to the sun and birdsong echoed from cliff face to cliff face in mysterious echoes, and ancient aborigines had painted their legends on the walls of cool caves. He had promised to show it to her sometime. He could not have meant it. Abruptly Karen reprimanded herself once more. She must stop this unhealthy preoccupation with Guy.

Linda's arrival made it easy for a time at least. Karen found her excitement mounting as she waited for the thrice-weekly plane to arrive. It was soon evident that Linda had been looking forward to the reunion just as much. She rushed into Karen's outstretched arms and they hugged each other.

'Wow, I made it!' cried Linda, breaking away and staggering comically. 'I never did like flying. I can't think what you see in it!'

Karen was surprised to find that her ebullient devil-may-care friend was nervous of flying. She picked up one of Linda's bags and led the way to the car.

'I bet you thought I'd chicken out at the last minute,' Linda said with a laugh.

'I didn't!'

Linda grimaced. 'It was a bit tempting to, I admit, especially as you don't know how long you'll be here. The outback and me—I'm not at all sure we'll get along.'

Karen glanced at her anxiously. 'Linda, I hope you haven't come just because of me?'

Linda squeezed her arm. 'No, I've got lots of other reasons!' She smiled a cryptic smile which Karen did not take too seriously and added, 'Besides, I'm as game as Ned Kelly and to parody that old familiar flykiller advertisement, when I'm on to something I stick to it!'

Karen pursed her lips. 'Yes, I know, and you wouldn't want to let them down, either, but I feel badly about it because you only agreed to come in the first place because of me.'

'Partly.'

'You're just trying to make me feel better,' said Karen.

Linda dumped her suitcase beside the car. 'Oh, come on, Karen, don't make a martyr of yourself over it. I'm here now and I'm going to stay.' She stowed her cases and then flung herself into the passenger seat.

'Whew! It's hot! I could use a nice cool shower.'

'You can have one just as soon as we get home,' promised Karen.

Linda was doing her hair after having had the shower and changed her clothes when she suddenly said to Karen, who was sitting on her bed watching her, 'Well, *you* ought to be

182

glad you came, Karen, in spite of the problems. It's done you the world of good. You've
filled out quite a bit in a fortnight and I haven't
seen you with so much colour in your cheeks
for ages. You've lost that dreadful stagnant
look.'

'Did I look stagnant?' Karen asked with a
laugh. 'Heavens, how awful!'

Linda grinned. 'Well, not all green and
smelly but you know what I mean, as if you
were never going to sparkle again. But ...' she
turned round and looked keenly into Karen's
eyes, '... I do believe you're getting a bit of
your old sparkle back. *You* evidently like the
job.'

Karen nodded. 'I do, very much, but ...' she
shrugged helplessly. 'It's only temporary.'

'Maybe I can persuade old Ogre Kendall to
let you stay,' said Linda with some levity.
'Wait until he feels the full force of my powers
of persuasion!'

Karen swallowed. She knew Linda was half
serious. 'I don't think ... well, I know you only
want to help, but on this issue I'd really rather
you didn't try to plead my case. His mind is
quite made up and he'll only think I put you
up to it.'

'Pretty formidable, is he?'

'He is ...' Karen was not sure how to describe

Guy accurately. She thought for a moment, then went on, 'He's very forthright and he doesn't tolerate interference or criticism or opposition to his decisions. For your own sake, Linda, don't antagonise him, especially not on my behalf. He can be very pleasant providing his authority isn't questioned.'

'Hmm,' murmured Linda thoughtfully, 'that's hardly promising news for the nursing profession's original rebel, is it?' She made a face. 'What's Matron like?'

'Oh, she's wonderful. You'll love her. She's terribly efficient—you have to be to work for Dr. Kendall—but she has a marvellous sense of humour and she's very kind.'

'So King Kendall is the only ogre around the place,' remarked Linda. 'Oh, well, it could be an interesting challenge. Maybe I'll try subtle tactics, like making him fall head over heels in love with me and then when he's putty in my dainty little fingers,' she demonstrated a squeezing action that made Karen laugh, 'I'll say no until he relents over you!'

Karen cautioned, 'I wouldn't advise that either, Linda. I suspect that Guy Kendall likes to do all the running after.'

Linda examined her fingernails critically. 'Oh, the way I operate, he'll think he is,' she said confidently.

Karen looked at her slim, suntanned figure. Linda was a graceful, willowy girl, like a young gazelle with her air of appealing gaucheness, but that concealed a very strong personality, a determined spirit and a bubbling generous personality. She might appeal to Guy Kendall, Karen thought, without any effort on her part. The thought of Guy chatting up Linda and kissing her friend as he had kissed her, suddenly made Karen feel oddly irritated. That evening as they were again in the bedroom they were sharing, changing before going to Dr. Kendall's house for the get-together, Karen said to Linda, 'I know it's a bit early to ask, but do you think you'll like it here?'

Linda paused from carefully touching up her toenails with bright red polish. She caught Karen's eye in the mirror. 'Well, I guess it's no worse than I imagined. The hospital seems okay and everyone I met was very friendly. Even Ma Carson seems quite a dear.'

Karen rolled the mascara brush over her long curving lashes. 'She is. I thought she was a bit of a dragon at first, but she hides her light under a prim exterior until she knows you, Miles said, and he was right.'

'I'm looking forward to seeing Miles again,' Linda said, screwing the top back on the bottle of nail polish. 'I hope he'll be able to get there tonight.'

'I expect so. We were just a bit unlucky missing him today. He had to go on a visit some way out of town.'

'He's nice, isn't he?' Linda said and treated Karen to a moment of sharp scrutiny.

Karen was ready for it. She had guessed that Linda would be wondering if a relationship had developed between her and Miles. She decided to be non-committal.

'He's very popular at the hospital,' she said. 'Everyone likes him. He's very easy-going.'

'Meaning they don't like Guy and he isn't?'

Karen was unaware she had emphasised the 'him'. She had not meant to.

'Not at all,' she amended quickly, 'but ... well, I suppose there is a slight difference. Guy is the Medical Director, after all. People respect him in a different kind of way but it doesn't mean they don't like him.'

'So it's only you who doesn't? Still I suppose that's understandable, considering the way he's treated you. I must say I'm dying to meet this monster.'

Karen felt remorseful. 'He's not really all that bad, Linda. We just don't see eye to eye on this pilot-nurse business, that's all.'

'You're still here,' observed Linda thoughtfully. 'He hasn't sent you packing yet.'

'Only because he hasn't found another pilot.'

Linda smiled. 'I wonder. Maybe he isn't trying. Maybe he's just too stubborn to capitulate decently.'

Her words stunned Karen. Could Linda have hit on the truth? Was Guy stringing her along, keeping her on tenterhooks, on purpose? Was this his revenge, punishment for the way she had treated him? Suddenly it seemed very possible.

As Mrs. Carson's house was not very far from the hospital and Guy's home just the other side of it, Karen and Linda walked the couple of blocks necessary to reach his place. The sky was aglow with a fiery sunset and the hot wind had dropped, leaving the air still warm with a faintly spicy smell drifting on it from some plant Karen did not recognise. There was almost absolute quiet except for the rhythmic sound of sprinklers turning on garden lawns. When they came to Dr. Kendall's house a babble of voices and soft music drifted out to them.

The party sounds came from the side of the house, so Karen did not bother to knock but pushed past the spreading hibiscus bushes which formed a hedge between the lawn and a pathway around the house. They emerged on to another lawn and the first person Karen saw was Miles. He was sitting on a garden seat talking to Kelly Maguire. He saw them at once, rose and walked across to meet them.

'Linda, great to see you again,' he welcomed, clasping her hands warmly.

'Good to see you, Miles,' said Linda, smiling, but a little subdued.

'I gather you were at the hospital for a little while this afternoon,' he said, 'but you didn't meet everybody.'

'No. I still have to meet Matron and Dr. Kendall who kindly arranged this gathering tonight,' said Linda. 'It was good of him to go to so much trouble.'

'No trouble at all.' The voice came from behind Karen and momentarily she felt light pressure on her waist as Guy moved in to stand between her and Miles.

He smiled at Linda and Miles introduced them. Karen was aware that Guy was absorbing Linda's appearance with expert masculine eyes and that she was making quite an impact. Maybe Guy was not so serious about Terri Lawson as everyone thought. Or maybe he was just a flirt.

Annoyingly, she again felt irritated at the thought of Guy falling in love with Linda. It was, she told herself, simply basic feminine pique because he was not likely to fall for herself. It was silly, because she did not want him to anyway, and there was no chance she would fall in love with him.

She turned her attention to Miles as Guy and Linda struck up a lively discussion almost at once.

Miles said, 'Looks as though they've made quite a hit with each other.'

'Oh, Linda's doing that on purpose,' Karen said.

'Jealous?'

Karen reddened. 'Miles, really! What a thing to say!'

'Stranger things have happened.' He turned his attention to Guy and Linda for a moment, then back to Karen. 'I'd say by the way she's looking at him it was instant impact. I don't know about him, though.'

'Linda is just flirting,' said Karen sharply. 'She always does. Didn't she flirt with you, too?'

Miles laughed. 'Come to think of it, I suppose she did. I wonder if Guy realises that's all it is.'

'He's a man of the world, isn't he? And a flirt himself, I gather.'

Miles took her arm. 'Let's leave them to it, shall we? I just heard him say he'll introduce her to everyone she doesn't know. They don't need us.'

They found a quiet spot and sat down with a drink, alone until Linda had done the rounds. There was a trickle of people coming and going and it was quite some time before she rejoined Miles and Karen. At the end of the evening Guy insisted on driving Linda and Karen home because Miles had gone back on duty. It was not very late and the two girls sat up talking for some time.

'Well, what do you think of Dr. Kendall?' Karen asked, brushing her hair while Linda sat on the end of her bed hugging her knees.

'Bit enigmatic,' said Linda, 'but rather fascinating. Those gorgeous grey eyes.'

'Sounds as though you've fallen for him!'

Linda shrugged. 'There'd be no point.'

'Why not? He looked interested.'

'Professional hypocrisy,' stated Linda forthrightly but without rancour, 'he was all the time thinking he would rather be with someone else.'

'My, you are a little psychologist,' said Karen, laughing, 'but you're probably right. There's a girl called Terri Lawson. You'll run into her in due course.'

'Hmm, well his mind wasn't totally on me anyway. He's already in love, I'd say.' She leaned towards Karen. 'And so, my dear

Karen, are you.'

'No, I'm not!' Karen was so startled she reddened, making her denial look false.

'Yes, you are.'

'Linda, please ... all this amateur psychology.'

'I know a lot about psychology and I know you, Karen Lalor. I've seen you in love and out of it and you're in love now.'

Karen drew in her lips and put down her hairbrush just a shade too forcefully. 'I am not in love,' she said clearly.

'The sparkle in your eyes tells me you are,' insisted Linda, 'and it was never more sparkly than tonight at Dr. Kendall's.'

'Now, you're being ridiculous. Dr. Kendall is the last man ...'

'Not him!' exclaimed Linda, bursting out laughing. 'I didn't mean him!'

'Then?'

'I thought there was a chance it might happen,' Linda said. 'Miles is a very nice man, Karen. You couldn't do better.' She sighed. 'I shouldn't have let you get a headstart on me!'

Karen was stunned. 'Linda, you mean that you ...'

'No! Only joking!' said Linda lightly. 'If he's the man for you, then I'm delighted. Now, I don't know about you, but I'm whacked. I'm for lights out.'

'Okay.' Karen switched off her light without pressing her denial that she was in love with Miles. She knew Linda would not believe her. It would do no harm to let her think it, for a while anyway. She lay awake thinking of all Linda had said, especially her insistence that Karen was in love.

Was she? Was she in love with Miles and didn't know it? She conjured up his face, open, kind, considerate, and was it sometimes tender, too? She did not know. Miles had helped her and it was not unreasonable that she should love him for it. But ...

Suddenly, behind the doubt came the realisation in a shock wave of horror. She knew that if she was falling in love with anyone, then it was with Guy.

'I can't be,' she told herself, 'it's crazy. I can't stand the man.'

Even as she mouthed the words silently in the darkness she knew they were untrue. He aggravated her unbearably at times but she didn't hate him any more. His touch had fired her as no other man's had. She had thought it could never happen again—but it had.

She knew now why she had felt irritated at the idea of him flirting with, falling in love with Linda. She was jealous. But it was too ridiculous. She could not be in love with a man who refused to acknowledge her as a competent person, able to do her job as well as any man. Guy would send her away when he felt he had punished her enough. He would find another pilot.

She sighed unhappily. The situation was worse than ever now and the realisation that love and hate were very close together on the emotional scale and that you could perhaps feel them both at the same time, was little consolation.

CHAPTER TEN

The first person Karen saw next morning in the hospital corridor after she had delivered Karen into Charge Sister Manning's care for her first day of duty, was Guy. He was walking towards her and there was no escape. Her throat constricted and she dared not look at him.

'Good morning, Sister Lalor,' he greeted her formally, stopping across her path so that she had no option but to pause also.

'Good morning, Dr. Kendall,' she answered politely, aware of a twinkle in his eyes.

'Someone is looking after Nurse Walters, I trust?'

Karen nodded. She wanted to flee and she wanted to rush into his arms. She could do neither. She had to stand there and wait until he decided to move. Her limbs felt rigid, her stomach a void and she could feel her temples pounding.

Guy looked sharply at her. 'Karen, are you all right?' His firm cool fingers touched her cheek. 'You're rather pale.'

The touch electrified her and she was sure his eyes, searching hers, would read the truth. 'I'm quite all right,' she faltered.

His hand gripped her shoulder. 'I hope so,' he said, and sounded genuinely concerned. 'We don't want you cracking up.'

Although his tone was kind she reacted angrily. 'Isn't that what you expect?' she shot at him. 'Isn't that what you're waiting for? So you're proved right?'

He seemed startled, then a smile flickered across his face. 'I guess you must be okay. You've lost none of your fire.'

'If you don't mind, I'd better get on with my work,' she said stiffly, shrugging her shoulder away from his grasp.

'By all means.' However, he did not let her go at once. As she made to pass him he pulled her back against him tightly, looked into her face with a burning intensity that made her pulses race and all her senses heighten, and murmured, 'You're a funny little girl, Karen.' Then he kissed the end of her nose.

Then as abruptly as he had caught hold of her he let her go and strode off down the corridor, leaving her trembling like a leaf in a storm. He was probably quite unaware of the havoc he was causing in her heart.

Each day was now an ordeal. Karen longed to see Guy, to have him near her, and yet she dreaded those moments until they came and felt totally drained afterwards because it was all so futile. At least that was what she kept telling herself, but deep down a small insistent voice kept arguing, 'He wouldn't flirt with you if he didn't like you. Maybe ...'

She would remember what Linda had said and wonder if perhaps Guy was not trying to punish her, that he meant to keep her on but would never actually say so. She wanted to believe it and she searched every encounter with him for some sign that his feelings for her were changing, but always she found only inconclusive evidence.

Sometimes she thought she had found tenderness, only to hear him ranting at her a moment later. She hated his arrogance and castigated herself for her foolish love. Whenever she saw him talking to another nurse she was jealous and it irked her most to see him with Linda. He seemed to get along better with her than anyone and was not as aloof as he usually was with others. Karen had to fight her jealousy hardest at these times because she loved Linda, too, and did not want to spoil their friendship. In self-defence she clung, metaphorically at least, to Miles.

A week or so after Linda arrived, Terri Lawson returned from a trip down south. Her arrival remained indelibly etched on Karen's mind because she appeared unexpectedly one afternoon at the swimming pool. Karen and Linda had been playing tennis with Miles and Guy, and Karen and Miles had won. Karen had not enjoyed it even though she had earned a word or two of praise from Guy for her backhand. Seeing Guy walk off the court with one arm thrown casually across Linda's shoulders as they laughed together about something had given her an all-too-familiar knife-thrust of jealousy.

Miles had wanted to swap partners for a return match, but Guy had demurred and said he would prefer a swim and a cool drink. So off they went to the swimming pool. Karen had not seen Guy in swimming trunks before and she found the experience painful. Her eyes were constantly drawn to look at his tanned and muscular body and she was forced to fight down the desire to be crushed hard against his broad lightly-haired chest. Unaware of her friend's anguish, Linda chatted and laughed and teased and sounded as though she hadn't a care in the world. Once or twice she looked knowingly from Karen to Miles and smiled at Karen in a secretive way.

Finally she suggested another swim. Karen could not bring herself to go into the water again where she might accidentally brush against Guy or be caught up in innocent but to her disconcerting horseplay, so she watched the others from the edge, her heart in knots. Guy seemed very relaxed, more relaxed than she had seen him, and she could not help thinking the reason was Linda.

Miles rejoined Karen after a few minutes. 'You know, I think Guy fancies Linda,' he said.

'Men usually do,' Karen pointed out. 'She's a very attractive girl.'

'So are you,' said Miles loyally. 'In a different way, though. She's an extrovert. You're quieter, harder to know.'

'And Guy likes extroverts,' said Karen. 'Take Terri for instance ...'

'No thanks!' joked Miles and on a sudden intake of breath added, 'Speak of the devil!'

Terri Lawson, Karen now saw, was approaching along the edge of the pool, glancing this way and that as though searching for someone. It could only be Guy. She walked with a swinging gait and was clearly aware of the admiring glances her progress evoked from the males sprawled near the pool. She looked like a model on a catwalk. Finally, she saw

Karen and Miles and tripped delicately across the grass towards them. At the same moment Guy and Linda emerged from the water, whether by coincidence or because Guy had spotted Terri, Karen could not guess. Terri saw them just as she was about to sit down.

'Guy, darling! So this is where you are!' She ran a few steps towards him and her voice tinkled like ice in a glass, Karen thought, Terri's gaze swept swiftly and disdainfully over Linda and made it clear that she was surprised to see Guy dallying with mere staff nurses. Karen was surprised, too, but his armour seemed to have fallen off quite a bit since Linda's arrival.

'I didn't know you were back, Terri.' Guy's eyes travelled over her with male expertise. The white bikini she was wearing showed off her curves and her tan to perfection. She had the enviable skin that was smooth and satiny with just the faintest dusting of fine hairs that gave it a peachy bloom. Everything about her was sensuous, Karen thought. It was no wonder Guy was keen on her.

'Sit down, I'll get you a drink,' he said.

'No, thank you, darling,' Terri said, glancing distastefully at the rest of the party, 'it's a little too warm for me outside. I'd prefer to drink in the lounge if you don't mind.' She swung the yellow cotton cape she was carrying over her shoulders. The fringe just covered the bottom half of her bikini.

Guy looked at the others in turn. 'Anyone else like to cool off inside?'

Linda looked a bit stunned and for once said nothing. Karen glanced at Miles, who said, 'Maybe we'll join you presently, Guy.'

Guy did not argue. He was probably relieved, Karen thought, not to have an audience for his reunion with Terri.

Karen felt as though a ton of bricks had been unloaded in her stomach. Looking at Linda she had the feeling her friend felt something of the same. Guy had been fooling around with both of them only because Terri was absent.

As the two walked away Linda let out a long breath. 'Boy, has she got him on a short piece of string.'

Karen murmured softly, 'I did warn you, Linda.' She hoped Linda had not fallen so heavily for Guy as she had herself.

Linda grinned impishly. 'If it weren't for the heat and my diminished energy after that tennis match, I'd join the battle, but ...' She stretched her long slim legs luxuriously and closed her eyes. Only Karen heard her murmur, 'I guess I'm a good loser really.'

Miles exchanged a look with Karen as

though to say, 'She's taking it well.'

Linda opened her eyes. 'Mind you, I wouldn't like to bet he cares as much for her as it looks.'

Watch it, Linda, Karen thought, you're kidding yourself just as I've been doing.

Miles said, 'They've been buddies for a long time.'

'Exactly,' said Linda. 'That's what it looks like except your choice of word, Miles, was perhaps a bit prim!'

Miles laughed. 'Maybe. I guess Guy's no angel.'

'What man is?' retorted Linda. 'I bet you're not so innocent yourself, Miles, dear. Is he, Karen? You ought to know!' she added mischievously.

Karen blushed and Miles looked a trifle discomfited. The embarrassment was, however, quickly dissipated by the sudden reappearance of Guy. He had left his towel behind.

'Come and join us now?' he invited. When they still looked doubtful, he insisted. 'My shout. Come and have a drink. It's turned into quite a party.'

This persuaded them. They picked up their towels and Karen donned a check shirt over her swimsuit. Linda thrust her head through her poncho and Miles threw on his shirt. A few moments later they joined the party in the Club lounge. Terri was holding court in the centre of a group of men. By the American accents and safari suits, cameras, spectacles and cigars, Karen guessed they were tourists. One was holding forth about a trip he'd made by Land-Rover. Guy drew up a chair for Karen and then, rather to her surprise, sat beside her.

'Oilmen,' he whispered. 'Big noises from the States, as if you hadn't guessed!' His eyes were humorous. 'Prototypes! We've got Ockers, they have these guys!'

'What are they doing here?' Karen asked, wondering if Guy was jealous of the attention Terri was commanding.

'Part of a prospecting team. They don't do any actual work, I gather, they're just the ones with the money to invest and they want to see at first hand where it's going. They've been filling in their time hunting.'

'Big game!' exclaimed Linda, who had heard what Guy was saying. 'Here?' She had not seen a single wild animal yet.

Guy's face set grimly for a moment. 'Some people will shoot anything that moves. There are emus and kangaroos, of course, there are camels and I suppose if you can't find any of them there are always crows and snakes.'

'You sound as though you don't approve of

hunting,' Karen commented. 'Do you?'

'Only with a camera, or if necessary for food.'

Linda leaned further across from the other side of Karen. 'If you've got a good cause going, Guy, just mention it to Karen and she'll join in. She's saved the whale, a couple of antique aeroplanes and heaven knows what else. Champion of the underdog is Karen.'

Guy was laughing. 'Truly!'

Karen felt embarrassed. 'I'm keen on conservation but it isn't quite like Linda said.'

Miles claimed Linda's attention and Guy said quietly to Karen, 'I've got a very good camera. We'll have to go shooting some time. That gorge I told you about has some interesting wild life.'

Momentarily her heart leapt. Why was he returning to the idea of taking her to see the gorge? Swiftly she denied the involuntary joy that flooded through her. It didn't mean anything. She must not be foolish. She did not follow up his remark but glanced at Terri and the group of Americans and said:

'Who's the one with the biggest cigar? He looks to be running the show.'

'He is. That's Ruben Arnstein, millionaire

from Texas.'

'Who hunts girls as well as game?' Karen suggested slyly, giving Guy a close look. Terri was clearly basking in the attention the men were giving her.

Guy gave nothing away. He merely shrugged and said, 'Terri can take care of herself, and Arnstein hasn't caught anything so far on his hunting trips.'

Karen laughed.

It was more than a week later that Guy asked Karen to fly him out to Wirrumburra Downs. She had only flown him on emergency or clinic flights before, but this was to be a visit to his home station for purely personal reasons.

'I've got a few things to settle with Jim Brady,' he told her. 'He's been on the radio asking when, so I told him tomorrow. Is that okay with you?'

'Yes, of course. I'm on call any time, you know that. I have to be.'

'I know, but this is personal, not medical. You have the right to refuse.'

He knew she would not, of course. 'You're the boss,' she said. 'If you say we go, we go. It's your plane.'

He looked at her quizzically. 'We might just manage to fit in a trip out to the gorge. It isn't far. Bring your swimsuit.'

Her heart began to race. He had meant it. He really was going to take her there. But she must not let it mean anything—he was merely going to show her an aspect of the country he loved. It was a small kindness, that's all.

He said, 'What's the matter? You look as though you've got a pain. Your face is all screwed up.'

She had not realised that her passionate denials to herself would show.

'Sorry, I'm all right. I was just ... thinking, I suppose.'

He let it pass. 'Do you ride?'

'No, I'm afraid I don't,' she confessed reluctantly.

'That's a pity,' Guy said, 'but never mind, I'll organise something.'

She did not dare ask him what just then. She felt disconcerted and wanted to get away from his disturbing presence.

She did not tell Linda about the proposed sight-seeing trip since Linda might put a wrong construction on it, and as she was clearly enamoured of Guy, she would be hurt even if Karen assured her that it meant nothing, that Guy was merely honouring a promise he'd rashly made.

The next morning dawned bright and clear

as it almost always did. The sky was like an upturned blue crystal bowl, without a wisp of cloud to mar its brilliance. Karen felt light-hearted, even a little light-headed, and the prospect of a leisurely day ahead instead of the usual hectic emergency or clinic run was pleasing.

In the shower that morning she had told herself firmly not to make anything of it. Guy was going to the station on business and if there was time he would show her the gorge. There was nothing more to it than that. She must stop speculating and take things as they came.

Oddly enough that had been Sean's advice once, a long time ago. The night he had kissed her passionately, the night they had almost made love, and confessed they loved each other. She had asked, 'Where do we go from here?' because wanting things cut and dried was part of her make-up, patience not one of her virtues, uncertainty the thing she hated most. He had stroked her face tenderly and said, 'Who knows? Let's just take it from here and see, shall we?'

Now Sean was dead and she had learned that life could not be planned in the cut and dried terms she wanted. She just had to take it from here and see ...

Scott Brady met them at Wirrumburra Downs airstrip. 'Hi, Sister,' he greeted Karen cheerily. 'Bit of a joyride for a change.'

'Unless we get an emergency call in the middle of it,' she answered wryly. 'Things have been a bit too quiet this last few days.'

They drove to the homestead with Karen sandwiched between the two men as before, and again she was acutely aware of Guy's body pressed close against hers, the bumping and shuddering of the truck making him move involuntarily against her, tantalising her with his nearness. He chatted cheerfully to Scott about station matters, seeming unaware of his effect on her.

At the homestead Jean Brady welcomed Karen as warmly as before, and this time there was more opportunity to talk because the men had business to discuss and for once Karen was not needed in her capacity as nurse. She helped Jean wash up after morning coffee and then spooned out biscuit mixture Jean had made on to trays ready for baking while Jean busied herself with other tasks. It was pleasant to engage in these small domestic chores and Karen enjoyed the change of occupation.

'Do you like boiled eggs?' Jean asked, as Karen was straightening up from putting a tray of biscuits in the oven.

'Yes, I do.'

'Good, I'll put a couple in with your lunch.'

Karen realised then that Jean was packing a lunch. 'Are we having a picnic?' It suddenly occurred to her that they were all going to the gorge and irrationally she felt disappointment, because she had imagined she would be going alone with Guy.

'Only you and Guy,' Jean said, and added with a laugh, 'He won't want any of us playing gooseberry, I'm sure!'

Karen was now embarrassed. 'Really, Jean, you wouldn't be ...'

'No? You like Guy, don't you?'

'Yes, but not ...'

'And hospital life doesn't give you much room for privacy, I know. Make the most of it, dear. Have a nice quiet day all to yourselves while you've got the chance. Guy doesn't often take a day off. You're very favoured!'

Karen took a deep breath. She was sure that Jean was jumping to conclusions, even worse ones than she herself had been guilty of. Before she could argue with the manager's wife about it, Guy came in.

'Nearly ready, Jean?' he asked. 'Jim and I have sorted out that little problem.'

'Yes, just,' said Jean, closing a plastic container. 'There,' she stowed it all into a large bag, 'not too weighty but plenty to eat. And don't bring a crumb back!'

'We'll feed what we don't eat to the fish,' he joked, 'rather than incur your wrath. Ready, Karen?'

Karen brushed the flour off her hands and untied Jean's apron. Jean said, 'Karen's been a great help.'

Guy slid her a faintly mocking smile. 'Domestic, too?'

'Very,' said Jean. 'She'd make a good station owner's wife.'

Guy asked laconically, 'Are you match-making, Jean?'

'I'm sure I don't need to,' she answered, while Karen writhed in embarrassment.

Guy laughed and turned to Karen, 'Come on, let's go.'

She followed him out to the shed where both horses and vehicles were stabled. She expected, after her admission that she did not ride, that he would take the utility or the four-wheel drive she had seen there, but to her surprise Scott was leading out one of the horses as they arrived, a huge black animal with a startling white blaze on his forehead.

He gave Karen a saucy look. 'Watch this fellow,' he warned, 'he's dynamite sometimes!'

She wondered if he meant Guy or the horse.

209

'I ... I don't ride,' she confessed nervously. Surely Guy did not expect her to learn today. Or—the thought sneaked in—was this his idea of more punishment?

'You are today,' said Scott with a grin. 'That right, Guy?'

'Sure thing,' said Guy. To Karen's surprise he mounted the big black horse himself. Briefly she wondered where that left her. She soon discovered. 'Give her a leg up,' Guy ordered.

Before she could protest she was being shot up in front of him to sit sideways in what seemed a very precarious position, at least it would have been but for Guy's arms holding her fast. He told her where to grip the saddle and when she protested he said, 'Well, you don't ride and there's no track for a vehicle where we're going, so unless you'd rather walk ...?'

Karen looked down. It seemed an awfully long way to the ground. Scott was grinning wickedly at her.

'Don't look so worried! He isn't carrying you off to his lair, only to a picnic in the gorge! Half his luck!'

Karen dared a quick glance at Guy. He burst out laughing. 'Good heavens, girl, you're not embarrassed, are you?'

She gritted her teeth. 'No, of course not. It's

210

just that I wasn't expecting ...' words failed her.

'Gee-up, Pharoah,' urged Guy crisply with a flick of the reins and the horse started forward at a slow walk. 'You'll soon get used to it,' Guy said to Karen. 'Comfortable?'

'Yes.' She was physically but emotionally she was in turmoil. Being forced to lean against him, almost enfolded in his arms, made her painfully aware all the time how she felt about him. At one stage they cantered for a short distance, but for most of the way Pharoah walked sedately along well-trodden dirt tracks into the hills behind the homestead.

'I wish I could paint,' Karen exclaimed involuntarily once. 'The scenery here ... it just cries out to be put down on canvas. It's so ... vibrant!'

In her excitement she caught Guy's eye and he smiled understandingly.

'My mother used to paint quite a bit. She was very talented.'

'Are those her paintings back at the homestead?' Karen asked. She had admired several in the hallway earlier that day and had meant to ask Jean who had painted them. They were obviously the work of someone who loved this harsh beautiful country as much as Guy did.

Now, Karen wanted very much to ask about

211

Guy's mother but she did not. She sensed that this was a private and personal area into which she must not intrude. She did not want to spoil the day by saying the wrong thing.

The further they went the more she relaxed. The rhythmic clopping of the horse's hoofs on the dusty track, the gentle swaying motion, took the tautness away and she began to enjoy her surroundings fully. Eventually, the hills loomed larger above them and the path twisted and turned many times until at last they squeezed through a narrow opening between two huge misshapen boulders. On the other side a breathtaking view met Karen's astonished eyes. Between two sheer cliffs flowed a river, still as polished glass in its wider parts, rippled in other places, and just below them rushing over jagged rocks in a noisy waterfall.

'It's beautiful,' she breathed, 'just like you said. I hadn't imagined it quite like this.' After the starkness of the country outside, this oasis was like a mirage.

'Okay, Pharoah,' murmured Guy and obediently the horse walked slowly down the path to the water's edge. There was an eerie stillness about the gorge and the silence was broken only by the rushing of the waterfall and the occasional bird call.

Guy drew rein near the water's edge where a couple of fallen tree-trunks jutted out into the water. He dismounted and held out his arms for Karen. Briefly he held her against him as she teetered between the horse and the ground, then steadied her roughly as though something had annoyed him.

Karen ran to the water's edge. 'The water's so beautifully clear.'

'It comes from springs. It isn't so clear after the rains, though. A real torrent bursts through here then, especially if there's a flash flood. Look, you can see where it has reached, right up there.' Guy pointed to the tide mark far above the present water level and Karen, picturing the flood pounding through between these sheer walls of rock, shuddered.'

Guy glanced at his watch. 'Hungry?'

She nodded, discovering that she was. 'Yes, I am.'

'Good, we'll eat now, have a swim later and we'll go home through the gorge and I'll show you the aboriginal cave paintings. It's the long way round but we'll make it before dark if we don't dally.'

'We'd better,' she said. 'No night flying allowed, remember. A sudden thought struck her. 'Guy, what if there's an emergency while we're out here? Someone would have to ride all

213

the way ...'

Guy pointed to one of the saddlebags. 'I've got a walkie-talkie, don't worry.'

'You think of everything, don't you?'

'I have to. Now, are you going to unpack the lunch?'

He spread a blanket on the ground in the shade and Karen opened up the sumptuous lunch Jean Brady had given them. There was enough cold ham, chicken, cheese, salad and pickles for four or more, but surprisingly they managed to eat most of it between the two of them. In the vacuum flask was iced coffee and in a small insulated box, fruit salad and cream.

'This is a banquet, not a picnic,' said Karen, lying back, satiated.

'Jean's a champion picnic maker,' agreed Guy, stretching out near her.

A pink and grey galah screeched as it flew across the gorge. Its call echoed from the sheer cliff faces and it sounded like answering calls.

Presently a kingfisher took up a station near the spot where they were sitting and captured their attention for some minutes as he dived after insects on the water. Later it was an eagle hawk soaring high above the sheer walls of the gorge and swiftly diving to snatch a prey.

Suddenly Guy touched Karen's arm, making her jump. 'Look ...!'

He pointed and she saw three kangaroos come down to the water's edge a short distance away to drink, unaware of them, unapprehensive of any danger. For a while it was as though they were invisible, and to Karen there was a timelessness about it as though they were transported back into some previous age. Impulsively, she said so to Guy.

'I feel like Stone Age man,' she whispered. 'As though the world has just been born.'

Guy did not laugh. 'It's good to feel like that sometimes,' he said softly. 'It's good to get one's feet back on the real earth, to be one with it even just for a little while, to be oneself for a change.'

She glanced at him in surprise. She would have thought he was always himself, utterly and completely.

His eyes helds hers and for a moment the whole world stood still. In her mind it was like a film that had suddenly stopped. Everything around her became frozen images. Not a breath of air stirred a leaf, the kangaroos were merely painted on a painted landscape of cliffs and ghost gums and shining water, everything was a mere trick of an artist's brush.

Then the film began to move again. Guy's arms enfolded her and his lips began to explore hers. The ground beneath her was hard and unyielding as his body pressed on hers, but she did not notice it. Her arms, with a volition of their own, twined around his neck and her fingers stroked his hair. There was nothing else in the whole world except the beating of Guy's heart against her own and the blood running fast and fiery in her veins.

Suddenly he lifted his mouth from hers, groaned slightly and looked at her through narrowed lids, his lips still parted and moist as were hers, tiny beads of perspiration glistening on his brow. He ran his fingers through her hair with rough affection. 'Karen, you little witch!' he breathed huskily. 'Why do I let you do this to me?'

Some imp of mischief made her say, 'We're not on duty!'

He laughed aloud and sat up. She felt forsaken so she sat up, too, hugging her knees, waiting for the turmoil inside to quieten. She looked warily at him, his strong profile outlined against the rugged cliff face, a man who belonged as much to this wild country as to the clean white clinical world of hospital wards, as much to the harsh glare of this summer sun as to the arc lights of the theatre.

She knew more certainly than ever now that she loved him, not just because of the strong physical attraction he had for her but for many other reasons, too. But did he care at all for her? What was a kiss? It could mean love to one, only passion to another. It was cruel that it had such wicked duality.

'Why don't we have a swim?' he suggested, and began unbuttoning his shirt.

Karen had worn her bikini as he had told her to and now she unzipped her slacks and stepped out of them, but reluctantly. Swimming almost naked with him would put a strain on her emotions and they were in turmoil enough as it was. Still, she followed him into the water, diving off a log at the place he said was safe from snags. The water caressed her perspiring skin like cool silk and the sun filtered through the surface in crazily dancing shapes. Small fish darted around her, their scales glinting in the sunlight.

They swam lazily for a few minutes, not speaking, keeping a distance from each other. Karen wondered if Guy was perhaps regretting the impulse which had fired him just now. She clambered out first and sat on the log dangling her legs in the water. He swam around for a while longer, his tanned muscular body cleaving the water like a fish. Then he pulled himself out and sat beside her.

'The echoes in the gorge are quite something,' he said. 'You heard that parrot?'

'Yes.'

'Call out. Go on, try it.'

She called out, 'Coo-ee!' The sound echoed eerily from the cliff faces, like her own voice trying to escape, she thought, and unable to scale the heights. Like her trying to escape Guy's spell while he kept pulling her back, cruelly enmeshing her.

He ran a finger down her leg from thigh to ankle. 'You have very sexy legs, Karen.'

'Good line, Doctor,' she joked, and removed his hand from where it encircled her ankle. She was going to have no more of his love-making. She could not trust him and even less herself. She was mad to have come on this picnic. Dr. Kendall was just a man like any other, and she a stupid fool.

'Karen ...?' He seemed puzzled, as well he might, she supposed, but she had made up her mind to be firm, with herself and with him. His hands clasped her waist and dragged her closer to him. She struggled as his lips roamed her neck, fighting the desire to give in.

'Karen, what's the matter?'

'I ... I don't think we should go too far,' she said, tugging at his hands.

He smiled and held her tightly against him so that her breasts in their thin cotton covering pressed hard against his chest and his legs imprisoned her thighs.

'I'm not going to take advantage of you,' he whispered. 'I promise.'

'No, Guy,' she said firmly, wondering where the willpower came from.

She wrestled herself determinedly from his grasp but he was not so easily deterred. He kept his hold on her and inevitably they lost their grip on the log and toppled into the water. The instant she was free Karen struck out for the bank, scrambled out ahead of him and raced up to where they had left their clothes. She swiftly pulled on her slacks and shirt and by the time he joined her she was packing up the picnic things.

He dressed in silence. Silently he strapped the saddlebags back on to Pharoah. Silently he lifted Karen into the saddle and silently he leapt up behind her. They rode home through the gorge but he did not stop to show her the caves or the paintings, and she had forgotten all about them, anyway.

They were within sight of the homestead before she spoke. 'I'm sorry if you're angry, Guy, but ...'

'I'm not angry,' he said curtly.

'Thank you for showing me the gorge,' she said. 'It's a very beautiful place.'

He did not answer.

In almost total silence they returned to Wirrumburra. When Guy dropped Karen off at Ma Carson's it was almost dark. In the glow of a fiery sunset his face was grim and he said a very brusque, 'Goodnight, Karen.'

'Goodnight, Guy,' she whispered, and ran inside, the tears poised on the brink ready to spill over.

Fortunately, Linda was still on duty so she was able to vent her misery in her pillow alone. It didn't matter now who had spoiled the day, Guy or her. All that mattered was that it had been spoiled. For a while she had thought they had understanding, some kindred spirit between them, but now she knew it had all slipped away.

'Oh, please, please find someone to take my place soon,' she begged the darkness. 'I can't stand it much longer.'

CHAPTER ELEVEN

After the disastrous day of the picnic, Karen tried as much as possible to keep out of Guy's way. Seeing him was painful. Of necessity they had to meet during normal hospital routines and several times Karen found herself assisting at operations he was performing. His manner towards her was always cool, aloof and strictly professional.

Those were the worst encounters. Watching him, she was always moved by his skill and dexterity and the very personal concern he showed for his patients. They were not just bodies needing repair, impersonalised by the paraphernalia of the operating theatre, they were always suffering individuals to Guy, she knew, whom he wanted more than anything to help. Of course, he knew many of them. Some were friends.

Guy was strictly impersonal with her, however. She had disappointed him and he was no longer interested in her, not as a woman, only as a nurse with a job to do. You didn't rebuff Guy Kendall and get off scot free. What had happened was her own fault, she knew very well, but it still hurt deeply that his interest had been so casual, that to him she had been just another potential conquest. If only she'd listened to her own good sense and not hoped for the impossible.

Karen dreaded the first emergency when she would have to fly Guy out to some remote spot and they would be alone together. When the first call came, however, he astonished her by not going himself, but sending Dr. Frinton instead.

'He needs the experience,' he said shortly, when he told her. There was a cynical gleam in his eyes as he added, 'I'm sure you'll enjoy his company more than mine.'

She had no answer to that. Her stomach felt as though tied in a knot and a wave of the old hatred washed over her as she looked at him, submerging, for a moment, her love.

On the next two occasions, Guy still did not go with her. Once Miles was rostered and then Lou Frinton again. Neither of them seemed to connect Guy's not going with Karen. Miles, in fact, was sure that their relationship was greatly improved.

'No sign of your replacement yet,' he commented. 'Looks as though Guy's letting it ride.'

'I doubt it,' she replied. Now, more than ever before, he was bound to be looking for a new pilot. Let it be soon, she prayed.

In between whiles she tried to forget about Guy and to suppress her feelings for him. She threw herself into every activity that was offering in her spare time. She swam, played tennis, and went to every party she was invited to. Mostly she and Linda, Miles and Lou made a foursome and there was usually much laughter and high spirits on the surface, but underneath it all Karen was longing for the day when she would no longer have to bump into Guy Kendall or work alongside him.

She saw him occasionally at social functions and always he seemed to be following her with dark censorious eyes. Always, too, he seemed to have the slim red-tipped fingers of Terri Lawson's hand along his arm, her fine gold hair brushing his cheek.

One night after a party when Karen and Linda were late home, Karen flopped on to her bed and uttered a deep sigh. She felt exhausted, not physically so much as emotionally. It was always like that lately.

Linda regarded her anxiously. 'Karen, you look washed out. Are you all right?'

Karen sat up. 'I think so! I'm just a bit tired, that's all. You must admit life is pretty hectic around here.'

Linda smiled with satisfaction. 'Yes, it is, isn't it?' Then she added quietly, 'You haven't quarrelled with Miles have you?'

Karen was astonished. 'No, of course not!'

'That's good. I just thought ... well, you've been a bit edgy this last few days.'

'I'm sorry, have I? It's probably just the heat.'

Linda nodded. She stretched out on her own bed. 'I feel a bit jaded myself sometimes. I don't think I'm going to last long up here, Karen. Do you think Guy will be terribly mad if I quit when you do.'

Karen rolled over to face her friend. 'Probably, but I wouldn't worry about it. They have a fairly rapid turnover of nurses here, I gather. What will you do? Go back to your old job?'

'If they'll have me.'

'I'd be surprised if they wouldn't.' She sat up again and leaned towards Linda. 'Linda, I'm sorry. It's all my fault you're here at all.'

'What utter rubbish!' exploded Linda. 'It's all *my* fault *you're* here. Now let's get to bed or we'll never be up in time in the morning.'

If Guy had deliberately sent Miles and Lou out on flights to avoid contact with her, Karen wondered what would happen on the next circuit. She could not imagine him leaving that to the other two doctors and she waited with nervous anticipation to see what would happen. He told her the night before.

'Clinic day tomorrow, Sister,' he stated crisply, encountering her in a corridor during one of his rounds. 'You haven't forgotten?'

'No, of course not,' she replied, forcing herself to meet his gaze levelly. 'I'll be waiting for you ready for take-off at the usual time, that is,' she added, 'unless Dr. Curtis or Dr. Frinton will be going instead.'

A cynical smile moved his lips. 'Would you prefer that?'

'My preferences have nothing to do with it,' she replied.

'You do, however, appear to find their company most congenial,' he pointed out. 'In a social sense at any rate.'

He was beginning to rile her. 'You don't object to my having a social life in my spare time, I hope,' she challenged coolly.

'Your life is your own to do what you like with,' he said. 'Tomorrow at eight, Sister, and don't be late. We have a tight schedule with a couple of extra calls to fit in.'

'I suppose one of the other doctors will be coming this time, too,' Karen said. There had always been two doctors on the circuit when

Alex Cable flew the plane, as well as a nurse, and the last time—Karen's memorable first time—Guy had complained about the pressure on only one.

Now he said shortly, 'No, they will not.'

He turned on his heel and left her without waiting for any response and Karen stood clenching her fists, wanting to hit him and at the same time longing for his arms around her whether his interest was casual or not.

A few moments later she glimpsed herself in a mirror in the nurses' room and was dismayed by what she saw. She examined her reflection more closely. Her face was pale and drawn. Her eyes looked larger and deeper set than usual and were dark-ringed. The lighting was not good, true, but it was not just that making her cheek bones prominent and drawing her mouth into a tense line.

'I must get away soon,' she thought. 'I'll ask him about my replacement tomorrow.'

She was as nervous the next morning as the first time she had flown Guy, pretending to be Alex Cable. She had had all night to brood over today's encounter and to try to project in her mind how it would be. If only Miles or Lou had been coming too, that would have lessened her ordeal. She wondered why Guy had decided to do the circuit singlehanded when by his own admission it was to be a more hectic one than usual.

She was on the runway ready for take-off when he arrived. He greeted her pleasantly enough but she sensed his withdrawal from her even though he sat beside her and not behind as she had half expected. They were in the air before he spoke again, and then it was to give her a surprise.

'We won't go to my place first today,' he said. 'We'll do the circuit in reverse order.'

She glanced at him. 'But won't they be expecting ...?'

'Everyone has been advised,' he said curtly. 'Nobody will be kept waiting, don't worry.'

She ought to have known that, of course. She wondered what had provoked this change of plan but did not dare ask. There was something aggressively purposeful about Guy today, she felt, and it made her uneasy. His face was set grimly.

It proved to be a long tiring day with the extra calls forcing them into a tighter schedule than before. There were also a few unexpected cases requiring longer treatment than most. Karen felt weary and tense, not so much because of the pressure they were working under but because of the perpetual close proximity of Guy. She was never away from his side for more than five minutes at a time. He spoke to her brusquely and only when necessary, and the day seemed endless. She could not help a long deep sigh as they approached Wirrumburra Downs at last.

To her surprise he said quite kindly, 'Soon be through now.'

It could not be soon enough for her. She went through the motions yet again when they arrived, assisting him automatically with the line-up of patients, the old men, the pregnant women, the children, some with black skins, some with white, all with ready smiles and thanks for the doctor and his nurse.

Some had real ailments, some had only fears to be allayed and some had little more than a touch of loneliness.

'Loneliness is as much a disease as any other,' Guy rebuked her, not harshly, when in a moment of irritation she remarked on the waste of time seeing patients with nothing wrong with them.

She realised he was right. There were people living out here for whom the regular visit of the doctor was the only milestone in their monotonous solitary lives. She marvelled at his patience and calm and the serious attention he paid to every word spoken to him. How could she not love a man who had won her admiration in spite of his callous treatment of her.

At the end of surgery, Karen was packing up ready to go, rehearsing what she was going to say to Guy about leaving, when he came back into the sleepout.

'Nearly ready,' she said, conscious as always of his irritation with time wasting.

'No rush,' he said, surprisingly, and when she glanced up questioningly he actually smiled. 'We're not going yet.'

'Oh?'

He walked into the room and grasped her shoulders. She shivered at his touch but did not try to shake it off. It was the first time he had touched her since the day of the picnic and she was caught off guard. She was also astonished to see the deep concern in his eyes.

'You look all in,' he said. 'You're not moving until you've had a rest.'

She was speechless for a moment. Then she faltered, 'I'm all right, really.'

'Rubbish. You're not flying another kilometre today.'

She recovered enough to be riled. 'If you're afraid I might drop off and crash you ...'

'Don't be so pig-headed, Karen,' he said, shaking her. 'You've been looking like death for quite a few days.'

She stiffened. 'I'm not tired,' she insisted 'and I'm not in the least unwell.' To give in would be a sign of weakness, and that was what he was always looking for, wasn't it?

'You've been overdoing it,' he insisted. 'Too many late nights. You haven't been getting enough sleep, and it shows.'

She looked away, chagrined. He was right, of course. She had thrown herself into a hectic round of social activities because of him, just to take her mind off him for as long as she could each day.

'I can still do my job,' she said. 'You have no cause for complaint about that, I hope.'

'No.'

'Well, then, let's get moving.' She turned and clicked shut the medical kit.

'You've got a date tonight with Miles, I suppose?'

She wheeled round to face him, angrily. 'I don't see what it has to do with you if I have, but as a matter of fact I haven't. I intend going to bed early tonight. I'm on in the morning and I knew today would be hectic, so I made no arrangements for tonight. I do have some common sense, Doctor!'

'And plenty of fire still,' he remarked, smiling wryly. 'But you're not on duty in the morning. I arranged with Matron for someone else to do your shift tomorrow.'

'You what!' She was outraged. 'You planned this ...'

'No,' he told her blandly. 'I radioed a few minutes ago. I told Matron we'd be staying here tonight as I didn't think you were fit to finish the flight back.'

'How dare you! I know whether I'm fit to fly or not.' She tried to push past him but his hands dropped on to her shoulders and held her firmly.

'Now don't get all hung up about it. It's no reflection on your stamina or ability or anything else.' He met her furious gaze calmly. 'I've got a few things to follow up from our last visit here and there won't be time to do that and fly back before dark as I had anticipated. If you insist on returning by yourself, by all means go, but it could make things awkward if there's an emergency requiring me and you'd have to return in the morning to fetch me.'

She was trapped. She had to do as he wanted. She drew herself up stiffly and quietly replaced the medical kit on the bench. 'All right. You give the orders. I have no alternative.' But deep down she knew he had planned this from the start. That was why he had not brought Miles or Lou, why they had done their circuit in reverse order.

Footsteps sounded on the verandah and Jean Brady knocked and popped her head around the door to tell them that afternoon tea was ready on the verandah. Karen meekly followed Guy out of the room.

Jean said, 'You're in the second room on the right off the hall, Karen. You'll find everything you want there and the bathroom is next door. I expect you'll feel like a shower later.'

'Thank you,' Karen said. 'I hope I haven't put you to any trouble. If I'd known ...'

Jean laughed. 'No trouble, my dear. We're used to unexpected guests.'

Guy's girlfriends perhaps, Karen wondered.

Guy motioned her into one of the cane loungers placed near a table on which tea was laid. He solicitously arranged a cushion behind her as she sat down and put her feet up. His softer manner puzzled her but she decided he must have got over his annoyance with her and the small dent she must have made in his masculine pride the last time they were here. She was a patient now, in a way, and patients always received the utmost care from Dr. Kendall. She sighed. It was a relief, but it did not change anything. She still had to tell him she wanted to leave.

He poured the tea and handed her a cup.

She found it difficult to avoid his eyes although she wanted to. They made rather stilted conversation for half an hour and then Jim Brady appeared and said he was ready, if Guy was.

Guy glanced at Karen. 'I'll see you at dinner,' he said. 'Jean's in the kitchen if you want anything, but I should just rest awhile if I were you.'

Karen nodded. Alone, she stared out across the now shadowy lawn towards the wide open spaces beyond. The hills were purpling in the glow of the setting sun; there was still a drowsy hum of bees in a creeper growing over the verandah and silver eyes were twittering in the peppermint trees. A magpie strutted across the lawn into the spray from the sprinkler and shook his feathers in the cooling water. Karen put down her empty cup and blinked once or twice. The rebel in her refused to admit she was tired. She would go and see if she could help Jean with dinner. She blinked again but the next time her eyes remained closed.

Karen did not remember falling asleep. She woke with a start and looked up into Guy's face, scarcely distinguishable in the gloom, for it was now almost dark. She saw what she felt certain was a smile of triumph on his lips. His diagnosis had been vindicated.

'I ... I must have dropped off,' she said,

sitting up abruptly.

'For a couple of hours,' he chided teasingly. 'For one who was not in the least tired you slept remarkably soundly.'

She was angry with herself and yet she had to admit she did feel refreshed. She had slept better out there on the verandah on the cane lounger than she had in her own bed for days. 'It was simply the heat, the tea and having nothing else to do,' she insisted, determined not to give in.

He laughed at her. 'Well, now you're awake, what about dinner? Jean's almost ready, she says. Want to have a shower first?'

'Yes, please!'

She swung her legs off the lounger. Guy grasped her hand and pulled her to her feet. She was uncomfortably aware of him and drew her hand away. She walked past him into the house, only pausing long enough to pick up her shoulderbag from the floor. She found the bedroom Jean Brady had made ready for her and entered thankfully. It was a small daintily-furnished room, very feminine, and overlooked the garden which she could, however, see little of in the darkness.

Karen drew the curtains against the night and undressed. Jean had thoughtfully laid out on the bed a dressing-gown, a fine cotton nightdress, a toothbrush, two towels and even a pair of scuffs. On a hanger on the outside of the wardrobe was a richly patterned kaftan in deep purple, green and gold tones. Karen was examining it when Jean tapped lightly at the door and came in.

'Karen, dear, are you feeling better now?'

'I had a good sleep,' said Karen with a laugh. 'But Guy is fussing a bit. I'm not about to crack up. He seems to think all women are frail little things without any stamina.'

Jean frowned. 'Does he? I wouldn't have thought that. He's always full of praise for the job you're doing and says you make far less fuss about it than most men would.'

Karen opened her eyes wide. 'Really! He said that? Oh, Jean, if only he'd say that to me ...' She stopped. What would it matter if he did? She still could not stay, even with his praise and approval. Not loving him. It would be impossible.

'You're ... fond of him, aren't you?' Jean suggested quietly.

Karen did not look at her. 'I admire him very much, Jean, that's all.'

Jean sighed. 'I must say I'd like to see him settle down, but ...'

'He prefers casual relationships,' Karen said with a touch of bitterness. 'He's not a one-woman man. He doesn't fall in love.'

'Harsh, words, Karen,' said Jean in surprise. 'I don't think you're quite right. I'm sure Guy doesn't prefer casual relationships, but always something seems to stand in his way, at least so it seems to me.'

'What do you mean exactly?'

Jean sat on the end of the bed, toying with the edge of the counterpane.

'I think he's afraid to fall in love, my dear, terribly afraid.'

'Why should he be afraid?' Karen was intrigued by this unexpected view. Jean lifted her shoulders in a despairing gesture. 'Because of his mother and sister, I believe.' She looked straight at Karen. 'Has he told you much about his family?'

'No. I know his parents are dead. I didn't know he had a sister.'

'He doesn't talk about any of them much. You see, when his father died Guy was away in London. He didn't come home immediately because he was at a crucial time in his studies. His mother carried on alone but she had an unsuspected heart condition and it seems she overdid things and collapsed—this was before Jim and I came here. She recovered but she didn't tell Guy about it. Well, it was presumed that another heart attack was what caused her to crash.'

'Crash!' Karen was startled.

'She used to fly a lot. She was quite a character, I believe. Well, when she died Guy came home and I don't think he's ever forgiven himself for not being here after his father died to take the burden off her shoulders. They were very close, mother and son, and he was close to his sister, too, very protective of her, so I've been told. Mary was apparently a very frail child. She died when she was sixteen. She had wanted to be a doctor, too. I think Guy feels somehow responsible, that being a doctor he ought to have been able to save her. But of course he couldn't. It was leukaemia.'

Karen felt tears pricking her eyelids. 'He's had a tragic life,' she murmured.

Jean nodded. 'It's been hard for him, but he isn't the kind of man to sit around pitying himself. He flung himself heart and soul into his work, but I have this feeling that he's afraid to fall in love. The two women he had loved deeply, his mother and his sister, both died. Perhaps he's afraid that a third ...'

'But that's superstitious,' broke in Karen.

'We are all superstitious sometimes,' said Jean quietly. Then she jumped up. 'But I didn't come to depress you. Don't ever let him know what I've told you, will you? I may be quite wrong. And now, before the dinner spoils I'd better get back to the kitchen and let you change. I left the kaftan out for you if you feel like something cool and unrestricting to wear. I thought you might be able to relax better in it than in the shirt and slacks you've had on all day. I bought several when we were in the Middle East for a holiday last year, a bit daring at my age, I suppose, but they are so cool and comfortable in this climate. I haven't worn that one yet.'

'It's very kind of you,' Karen said, 'but ...'

'Please wear it,' urged Jean. 'I'd like you to. And I'm sure Guy would, too!'

Karen smiled. 'Well, I do feel a bit crumpled and crushed, so I will. Thank you.' But not to please Guy, she thought.

'And use any of my cosmetics and perfume you want,' Jean added generously, waving her hand towards the dressing table.

When the manager's wife had left, Karen hurried into the bathroom and took a tepid shower. She felt very refreshed afterwards and was glad, too, she had agreed to wear Jean's kaftan. They were about the same size so it fitted her perfectly and it was soft and cool, allowing the air to circulate around her body. For extra coolness she pinned her hair back behind her ears but did not bother to apply any

238

make-up other than eye-shadow and a touch of lipstick. Her eyebrows were fine and dark and needed only occasional shaping. She licked her finger and smoothed them deftly into their naturally arching lines. She hesitated a moment over Jean's bottles of perfume, then recklessly sprayed a little of one of her own favourites on her neck, wrists and between her breasts.

Guy was in the hall as she emerged from her room. She felt his eyes roving casually over her with undisguised approval after his initial surprise at seeing her dressed up.

'It's Jean's,' she explained, smoothing the dress. 'She thought it would be cooler for me.'

'It suits you,' he murmured, 'and so does the perfume!'

Their eyes locked briefly. There was no mockery in his, she was glad to see. She looked away again quickly, afraid that he might see too much of her feelings in hers. Inside she was filled with compassion for him. If only he would let her love him ... not just physically but wholly and utterly, loving, cherishing and ... she smiled to herself ... yes, even obeying!

As they sat down at the dining table, Guy murmured, 'I believe I promised to take you out to dinner as payment for typing that article of mine. It's going to be published, by the way.'

'Oh good, I am glad.'

His eyes were glinting with humour now.
'And as Jean's cooking is better than any in
town, we're in the best place.'

'Save your praise until after you've eaten!'
said Jean, coming in at that moment with a
delicious-smelling chicken on a bed of saffron
rice and a dish of mixed vegetables consisting
of carrot rounds, french beans, chunks of
aubergine and green and red peppers, tiny
onions and rounds of courgette. There was also
roast pumpkin, the brilliant orange flesh con-
trasting vividly with its bluey-green skin, and
appetising julienne potatoes. Karen suddenly
felt very hungry.

The meal ended with a cool sharp fruit salad
piled high with lime-flavoured ice cream, and
when they had finished Guy suggested they
return to the verandah for coffee. He told
Karen to go ahead and he would fetch the tray
to save Jean the trouble.

Karen walked out on to the verandah, feeling more relaxed than she had for some time.
She was glad Jean had talked to her. She had
a feeling the manager's wife was right about
Guy. It was sad but she could understand
perfectly how he must feel. She had suffered
in a similar way herself, even blaming herself

for Sean's death, and yet suddenly her grief seemed very small and insignificant compared with Guy's. She was not angry with him now for trying to use her.

She was so absorbed in her thoughts, and in the stillness and beauty of the night, with its myriad stars and dark velvet shadows, that she was not aware of Guy placing the coffee tray on the table, only of his presence when he stood right behind her and his hands slipped around her waist and his face brushed against her hair.

'It's a beautiful night,' she murmured shakily.

'And you're a beautiful woman,' he whispered, his lips close to her ear.

He turned her into his arms and his mouth touched hers, moving against her lips with such exquisite gentleness that it stirred every fibre of her being even more urgently than rough passion. She knew she should push him away but she could not. His power over her was too great. She had no will-power left where Guy was concerned and suddenly she didn't care whether he knew it or not. She only cared about loving him and being in his arms.

As he raised his lips from hers for an instant she whispered anxiously, 'Jean ...'

'Is a very discreet lady,' he murmured and

touched her lips with his fingertips. Then he kissed her again, slowly, persuasively and with increasing passion.

After a few moments he held her a little away from him and looked hard at her. 'Aren't you ashamed of being unfaithful to Miles?'

She was stung. She had not expected such a remark. 'I'm not being unfaithful to Miles!'

'No?'

'Miles and I are just good friends.'

His fingers tightened on her arms. 'Is that true?'

'Of course it's true! I like Miles very much, but there's nothing ... romantic ... between us.' She turned out of his embrace as his grip relaxed. 'The coffee's getting cold.'

'I like cold coffee,' he said, 'but ours happens to be in a thermos jug, so it can wait all night if need be.'

'I'd like some now,' she insisted.

He pulled her forcefully back into his arms. 'Karen, I blundered the last time we were here. I'm ... not very good at this sort of thing and there were ... oh, hell, I thought it was because you and Miles ... and I haven't been particularly kind to you and you must hate me ... but what I'm trying to say now is, I'm sorry. I find you the most beautiful, desirable woman I've ever met and you fill my thoughts as no one else has ever done, damn you, so ... Karen, each time I've kissed you you've led me to believe that you're not entirely indifferent to me.'

She was so stunned she could think of nothing to say to him. His outburst was so unexpected and her head was whirling, her heart pounding and she felt she might crumple into a heap at his feet if she didn't sit down. She had to take it in a little more slowly.

'Let's have coffee,' she managed to whisper.

She ran to the table and busied herself pouring out the coffee. She twittered nervously about milk and sugar and then handed him his cup with trembling fingers, not in the least succeeding, she knew, in covering her confusion.

He sat down and drank his coffee without speaking. Hers was hot and black and burnt her lips, but she tasted only the sweetness of his kisses.

He put his cup down. 'We started off badly, Karen. It was my fault.'

'It doesn't matter now,' she said. She didn't need him to apologise.

He crossed to her lounger. He gently took the cup from her hands and put it back on the table. Then he sat beside her and held her two hands in his.

'Presently,' he said, 'I'm going to talk. I've

got a lot of things I want to say to you, but at the moment all I want to do is this ...' He kissed the tip of her nose and ran his fingers through the thick coppery tresses of her hair, then kissed her ear and whispered, 'Karen, I love you very much. I want you to be mine.'

She was silent. Words seemed irrelevant. She could only show him how much she loved him. She lay back in his arms and felt his face next to hers on the cushions. His lips sought hers as his body pressed closer against her, closer even than the cane arms of the lounger insisted. She could smell faintly the warm tangy masculine sweat that dampened his shirt and she could feel every line of his body through the thin material of the kaftan.

His hand caressed her breasts through the material, but as his kisses became more urgent he soon became dissatisfied and slid his palm through the slit at the throat of the dress, gently eased the strap of her bra over her shoulder and his fingers closed warmly, excitingly over bare flesh. She felt the nipple press hard against his palm and a shiver of excitement ran through her.

He whispered urgently, 'You do love me, Karen. You can't deny it now.'

'No.'

'Let me hear you say it. Say you love me.'

'I love you, Guy.'

A cicada high in a tree started a lone aria. Guy's lips moved hungrily against Karen's. His legs gripped hers, moving against them forcefully, but suddenly the spell was shattered and Karen was aware of a voice intruding.

'Guy ... Guy ... are you still out there?'

It was Jean. Karen saw, in a daze, her dark figure outlined in the light behind the flyscreen door.

Guy leapt up as though he had been scalded. 'Yes, what is it?' Karen was dimly aware of his unbuttoned shirt, of her own disarray, and then more urgently she was alert to what Jean was saying.

'The hospital, Guy. There's an emergency at Dimboora Hills Station. A stockman was thrown from a horse and kicked. They've only just got him in and it seems he's in a pretty bad way. They're afraid he won't last till morning. Can you possibly go tonight?'

Guy glanced down at Karen. 'We've got to move, and fast.' Then he stopped, ran agitated fingers through his hair. 'Can you fly at night?'

Karen took a deep breath. The plane was not really equipped for night flying, but in matters of life and death ...

'Yes, of course,' she answered promptly. It was no time to worry about rules, or doubts even. Thinking swiftly she said, 'We'll need lights to identity the strip. Flares ... car lights ... anything to guide me in.'

'Jean?' Guy said.

The manager's wife nodded. 'I'll get through to Dimboora and alert them.'

'I'll have a quick word, too,' said Guy, and grim-faced followed her into the house.

While he and Jean contacted the station on the transceiver set, Karen rushed to the room she was to have slept in and changed back into her slacks and shirt. She grabbed her shoulder-bag and ran to the surgery at the end of the verandah to pick up the medical kit.

Jim Brady had the truck's engines running as she ran down the verandah steps. Guy was only a stride behind her.

'You'll have light,' he said briefly.

Karen glanced up. 'Fortunately there's a moon, almost full.'

Behind them as they raced along the rugged track to the Wirrumburra Downs airstrip came two other vehicles to provide extra light for take-off. In the eerie blue moonlight, with every pebble throwing a long shadow, Karen warmed up the plane's engine. The lights of the trucks were switched on and the strip stret-ched ominously ahead of her like a stretch of moon surface. She had not flown at night for a long time and this plane did not have instruments for night flying. Her heart thumped a little as they moved forward. The sky looked black and alien, the stars momentarily extinguished by the glare of headlights. Karen gritted her teeth. A man's life hung in the balance. It was no time to be afraid.

The moments of tension passed as she felt the aircraft lift and the ground fall away. The familiar and reassuring roar of the engine filled her ears as the little plane carried them high into the night sky. Soon there was only blackness below, and above a dusky starlit sky and the cold silver moon. Turning right, Karen glimpsed the homestead briefly, a few far-off twinkling lights and the moving firefly lights of the trucks returning along the track. As she levelled out after climbing, only then did her thoughts return to half an hour ago.

How happily she had lain in Guy's arms! The furthest thought from her mind was a mercy flight to the middle of nowhere. She glanced at him beside her, staring into the darkness ahead, and wondered if he, like her, was thinking that perhaps it was just as well the night had ended this way after all.

CHAPTER TWELVE

It was the early hours of the morning before
Karen finally fell into bed. She was glad she
had slept a little at Guy's place because there
was no chance of her sleeping now. The dash
to the injured man, the flight back to Wirrumburra in the dark, the strain and tension of it
all had keyed her up to fever pitch. Fortunately, she did not have to go on duty in the morning. Guy had seen to that previously, for his
own ends, and for this she was now grateful.

She could simply lie in bed and let last night
wash over her again and again, not the
emergency, but Guy saying he loved her.
Surely he would not have said it if he had not
meant it. Surely he would not have been
jealous of Miles unless ...

Jean Brady's words echoed in her mind. She
might be right—Guy had been afraid to love,
but perhaps that had been partly because he
had not met someone ...

Now he loved her. He had said so. She
wished she could have heard all the other

things he had promised to say to her but they would have to wait.

When Linda saw Karen in the morning she was all agog to hear about the emergency flight. To Karen's relief she brought good news about the patient.

'He'll live,' she said succinctly, peeling off her uniform. 'Guy's a bit of a whizz in the theatre, isn't he?' Her admiration was very plain.

Karen nodded. 'Is he still there?'

'Yes, I heard Matron trying to shoo him off just before I left. He looked all in. But the man's okay. He's got a head injury and a broken collar bone but luckily only minor internal injuries. It looks as though the horse kicked him.'

'It did. And he had a rough ride back from the camp to the station homestead in the back of a Land-Rover. He looked pretty far gone when we picked him up.'

Linda nodded. 'I know. I was there when they brought him into the theatre. I confess I'd written him off until Guy started on him.'

'I wanted to stay,' Karen said, 'but Guy wouldn't let me.'

'I should think not,' said her friend. 'You looked about as bad as the stockman. Bit hair-raising was it, flying at night?'

'It was a bit,' Karen admitted, and told her about it. 'I didn't want to give Guy the willies so I didn't tell him I hadn't flown at night for a long time and then only a few times with Sean. It's very easy to get disorientated at night. I've heard of people flying upside down and not knowing it. The people at Dimboora Hills Station were great, though. They must have rustled up every light in the place short of candles. It was fantastic. One minute there was just this awful blackness where I was expecting the airstrip to be and I was sure I must have gone terribly wrong somehow, and then suddenly dead ahead the lights all came on together. They waited, of course, until they heard our engine. It looked like a fairground!'

'I bet you were relieved,' said Linda. That Karen actually enjoyed flying was beyond her.

'Not as much as Guy was, I expect!' murmured Karen, wryly.

'Well, it should count as a big mark in your favour.'

Karen just smiled. Marks in her favour were no longer necessary. Suddenly the implications of Guy being in love with her began to sink in. She would not have to leave. There would be no necessity to find a replacement for her. She would be staying here with Guy ... forever ...

'You look a bit dreamy this morning,' observed Linda. 'I suppose Guy gave you a sedative last night.'

'I suppose he did ...' Karen answered cryptically.

'He must have given you an overdose. What was it?'

'Oh, I forget ...' murmured Karen. 'It was very effective anyway.' She felt warm and happy but she did not want to tell Linda the news yet. It was still all too dreamlike and she wanted to see Guy again first, to reassure herself of the reality of all that had happened.

While Linda was preparing for bed, Karen rose and showered and dressed. As she was not on duty at all today she decided to relax at the Club swimming pool. Linda was already asleep when she returned from the bathroom, so she told Ma Carson where she was going.

'Ask her to join me there later,' she said, 'if she feels like it.'

'You had quite a night last night, I believe,' remarked Ma Carson.

Karen gave her a brief résumé of what had happened. 'And the patient is doing well, so Linda says,' she finished.

'And you look perkier than I've seen you look for some time,' observed Ma Carson astutely. 'You've been moping around like a lovesick hen for weeks.'

Karen laughed. 'Goodness! Is that what I've looked like?'

'Maybe he's asked you to marry him at last,' suggested Ma Carson slyly.

Karen was not prepared to give too much away. 'Not yet, but soon, I hope.'

Ma Carson sighed happily. 'Ah, well, he's a nice young man. Not quite cut out for the north, though, I'd say, but not everyone is.' She went on, 'I must say I'll miss him when he eventually goes south again. Dr. Curtis has always been a very cheery and polite person.'

Karen gulped. Ma Carson meant Miles! She escaped as quickly as she could before the conversation became too awkward, and on the way to the pool her conscience began to prick her a little as a result of what Ma Carson had said. Had she unwittingly encouraged Miles too much?

She was lying on the grass just beyond the edge of the swimming pool and just outside the shade cast by the umbrella fixed in the centre of a nearby table, deepening her tan and thinking guiltily about Miles, when a shadow fell across her like a cool touch of silk on her bare stomach.

She opened her eyes and looked up into Guy's. He smiled fondly at her and subsided on the grass next to her. He lay on his side, chin supported by one hand, and looked long and speculatively into her eyes.

'Busy night last night, Sister,' he observed, a twinkle in his eyes.

'Certainly was, Doctor,' she replied. Her heart was beating wildly and her body tingled just to have his eyes moving over it.

'You did a magnificent job, Karen.'

'That praise applies more to you.'

He chuckled. 'I suppose mutual back-slapping is better than quarrelling.' His eyes twinkled. 'Although I shall miss the fireworks!'

She started, 'Guy ...' She wanted to ask him to say now what he had been going to say to her last night. She had a feeling that he had wanted to talk to her about his mother and sister, his father, and perhaps even about marriage. She wished he would do it now so that she could be sure.

'Yes?'

Suddenly, she was unable to ask. It had to come from him, naturally, at the time when he wanted to. Here, beside the pool, with others around, was possibly not the right place. Guy might prefer privacy, the closeness and intimacy of just the two of them, and she knew she would prefer that, too. She must curb her impatience for once.

'Nothing ... I was just thinking ... about last night.'

He spread one hand across her belly. His fingers moved experimentally across the flat plane of her stomach. But he said nothing, only looked at her from time to time with a glance that set her pulses racing. For a few moments they lay there, silent, contemplative, Karen content just to be near him, and then suddenly he took his hand away. A moment later she saw why. Miles sat down beside them, unaware that he had broken any spell.

They all had a swim and presently Guy left them, saying he was going back to the hospital to check on his patient.

'You can't have had much sleep,' Karen said, concerned.

'Enough. I'll make up for it some other time.' He caressed her briefly with his eyes since no other way was possible then with Miles looking on.

'He's got a constituion like an ox,' said Miles, as Guy walked away from them. 'No wonder he expects a lot of other people.'

Karen hardly heard him. She was too far away in her thoughts.

'Karen ...'

Miles' voice, sharply, brought her back and she turned to face him. 'Mmm.'

'You're in love with him, aren't you?' The question was so unexpected that she was unprepared and it was clear from the way Miles was looking at her that her face had given her away. It would be pointless to deny it now, and why should she? Soon everyone would know.

'You're too smart, Miles,' she whispered.

He chuckled. 'And relieved.'

'Relieved?' She sat up, surprised.

'Ma Carson has been convinced for some weeks that you're in love with me. I've been trying to think what to do about it.'

It took a moment for Karen to realise the significance of what he had said before. 'And ... you're relieved ... because I'm not?' she said slowly. If he was relieved then it must mean he was not in love with her. Now it was Karen's turn to feel relief.

He said quickly, 'No offence meant, Karen. I mean ... well, at first maybe I did think you and I ... but with some people one is always just ... friends ...'

Karen smiled fondly at him. 'Miles, dear, you're not offending my feminine vanity or anything else. But there's obviously someone you're in love with. May I know who?'

His face changed. The corners of his mouth turned down and he looked despondent. 'Not

255

much point. No future in it.'

'Oh, Miles.' Karen touched his hand. 'I'm sorry. Is she married?'

He looked startled. 'Good heavens no! What made you say that?'

'I don't know. When someone is unattainable they're usually married.'

'Or in love with someone else.'

'Yes, I suppose so.'

He did not offer any further information and Karen did not like to probe as the subject was a painful one. She sat in silence for a few minutes, not knowing what to say to comfort him. Eventually she said, 'Linda will be along shortly, I expect. She was sleeping when I left her, but I told Ma Carson where I was going.'

When Miles did not comment, she went on, 'Linda's fitted in very well, don't you think, Miles, seeing she would not have chosen to come up here but for me?'

'Very well,' he agreed. 'So has Lou Frinton. What do you think of him, Karen?'

'He's very pleasant. Quiet, basically, but I've seen him let his hair down once or twice, egged on by Linda!'

'I hadn't noticed he minded.'

Something in his tone made Karen ask in surprise, 'Miles, you don't think Linda and Lou ...?'

He gave her an odd look. 'I thought it was obvious.'

Karen was taken aback. Linda flirted with everyone. She had not thought she was serious about anyone yet. 'I must say I hadn't noticed.'

He smiled dolefully. 'You've been a bit preoccupied yourself, probably.' He pressed her hand. 'Is he in love with you?'

She nodded, and Miles said, 'I confess I'm astounded, and yet on reflection I'm not, I suppose. You're right for each other.'

Karen did not want to talk about her and Guy, not yet. She was also intrigued by the idea of Linda and Lou. 'Linda and Lou,' she repeated, 'I can't quite see it ...'

Miles was given no opportunity to answer because Linda appeared and flopped down beside them.

'Hi, kids!'

'Hello, Linda,' murmured Miles and Karen caught the tail end of the look he gave her friend, a look Linda did not see, and she knew instantly without any shadow of doubt who the unattainable girl was. Miles was in love with Linda. Oh, poor Miles, she thought.

'I'm going for a swim,' said Linda after a moment or two. 'Coming, you two?'

Miles rose. 'Okay, Karen?'

'No, I must be off,' said Karen. 'I've got

some shopping to do. I'll leave you now if you don't mind.'

'See you later!' Linda sped down to the pool followed closely by Miles and Karen watched them, wishing things could be different.

She sighed and walked up to the change rooms. Dressed again, she realised she felt rather thirsty, so she went into the bar and ordered a long cold lime and soda to set her up before she embarked on her shopping. It was as she was taking her first sip that she heard Terri Lawson's voice and realised with a start that she was standing next to the girl who, with her back to Karen, had not noticed her.

Terri was with two or three other girls, Karen noticed out of the corner of her eye. She hurried her drink, not particularly wanting to join them, but she could not fail to overhear what Terri was saying in a confidential but clearly audible tone.

'... We're taking the plane to Perth tomorrow and we're going to choose a ring and make arrangements for the wedding. Actually I'm going to announce our engagement at my birthday party on Saturday, so keep mum about it until then, will you? I want it to be a big surprise for everyone. You'll be brides-maids, of course!' There were vague murmurs

258

and then she went on, 'Oh, I'm so happy! You know, I got the shock of my life when he popped the question, although it was obvious all along that he was keen. Men do take a time to get around to some things, and then it seems they just can't wait!' She laughed her happy tinkling laugh and Karen hurriedly finished her drink and slipped away before her presence was noticed.

It was not until later that Karen admitted to the suspicion that Terri's conversation had planted in her. As she walked around the shops it began to grow, no matter how much she told herself not to be ridiculous, and that evening when Guy summoned her to his office just after she had gone on duty, she knew she had been duped.

Dr. Lou Frinton was also in Guy's office.

'Oh, Sister Lalor,' said Guy matter-of-factly as though there had never been anything between them other than formalities. 'I've got to go down to Perth for a couple of days. I'll be going on tomorrow's plane. Dr. Frinton will accompany you on any emergency that arises and Dr. Curtis will be in charge here. I'll be back on the next plane.'

His face told her nothing. He had just said he was going to Perth tomorrow on the plane. Terri was going, too. It was too much of a coincidence. Who else could she be getting engaged to? Karen knew there was no one. Terri Lawson had been throwing herself at Guy for a long time.

Karen knew now what last night and the picnic in the gorge and all the other little incidents added up to. Revenge. A wave of humiliation washed over her. How could he be so heartless?

'This is sudden, isn't it?' she managed to say, when Dr. Frinton had gone out before her.

Guy nodded. He seemed preoccupied, and no wonder! 'Bureaucracy,' he said briefly. 'I think I'm going to be hauled over the coals about something.' He allowed a faint smile. She knew he was lying.

'Is that all?' she asked coolly, moving towards the door.

He stood up, his look a shade quizzical. 'I hope you don't have any problems while I'm away.' He moved towards her. 'Take care, darling. I might not see you before I go ...' She stepped away from him involuntarily and his eyebrows rose. 'Aren't you going to say goodbye to me.'

'We're on duty!' she said stiffly. 'Goodbye, Guy. Safe journey.'

Before he could stop her she walked out,

260

closing the door swiftly behind her. As she sped along the corridor outside she saw everything quite clearly, including her own foolishness. Guy had led her on until she had finally confessed to being in love with him. It had been deliberate, cold-blooded revenge of the worst kind. How he must be looking forward to her humiliation when Terri announced her engagement!

Miles had warned her, she thought, and she had half believed him until Guy had finally subdued all her fears. His egotism, his arrogance left her breathless. He had had no doubt that he could make her fall in love with him. And last night ... if that emergency had not arisen ... She shuddered at the memory of how besotted she had been. She could only be thankful now that Fate had intervened to stop her making an even bigger fool of herself than she already had.

Karen felt as low as she had ever felt in her life. She would have to leave now, she knew, just as soon as she possibly could. She wished she could leave on tomorrow's plane, too, but that was impossible. Somebody had to fly the *Jabiru*. She could not just walk out. All she could do was decide to tackle Guy as soon as he returned and hand in her resignation.

She was so steeped in her own unhappiness

that it came as a shock when she arrived home after her shift to find Linda, who was also off duty, sitting on her bed in tears.

'Linda, whatever's the matter?' Karen asked, sitting down beside her friend, her own misery forgotten. Immediately Linda burst into fresh tears. It was so uncharacteristic that Karen was alarmed.

'Nothing,' said Linda, predictably. Karen guessed that something very serious was the matter.

'You'd better tell me,' she advised, 'or I shall badger you until you do. I've never seen you cry! What on earth has brought this on? You're not ill, are you?'

Linda sniffed and shook her head vehemently. 'No ... well, maybe I am ...'

'Linda, please, what do you mean?' Karen was anxious.

Linda spread her hands helplessly. 'I'll have to go, Karen, there's no other way. I'll have to go soon. I can't stand it much longer ... every day is agony.'

Karen was astounded. 'I know you said you probably wouldn't want to stay on after I left, but is it really that bad?'

Linda nodded.

'But why? You always seem to be having a good time and with everywhere air-conditioned the heat isn't all that hard to take ...'

'It isn't the heat,' Linda said weakly. 'Look, I'm sorry you found me like this ... it's nothing. I'll get over it.'

Karen slipped her arm firmly around her friend's shoulders. 'Linda Walters, you're going to tell me what's the matter or I sit here until you do!'

'Karen ... I can't!'

'Why not? I'm your best friend, aren't I? What can't you tell your best friend, for heaven's sake?' The suspicion that it was something to do with Lou Frinton crossed her mind. Only a man, surely, could make Linda this unhappy.

'That's just it ... it's because you *are* my best friend.'

Karen was beginning to feel cross with her. 'Well, what have I done?'

'You haven't done anything .. except to fall in love.'

Karen drew a sharp breath. So Linda had guessed how she felt about Guy—or Miles had told her—and she was in love with him herself, not with Lou Frinton as Miles believed. It was of course so natural that Karen closed her eyes in despair. Now she would have to tell Linda the truth—not quite all of it perhaps, but enough to show her how foolish it was to be in love with Guy.

She said slowly, 'Guy's going to marry Terri Lawson. They're annoucing their engagement at her birthday party. They've gone to Perth to buy a ring.'

Linda looked up, startled. A look of bewilderment crossed her face.

'What's that got to do with anything?'

Karen frowned. 'Well, everything ... if you're in love with Guy.'

'I'm not in love with Guy! Good grief! Is that what you think? Then ...' She stared, realising the implications. 'But I thought ... Karen, you're in love with Miles! You detest Guy!'

Karen closed her eyes. She did. She didn't. 'No ...'

Now it was Linda's turn to put an arm around her shoulders. 'Oh, no, don't tell me you fell for Guy after all. In spite of everything. Oh, Karen ... and he's going to marry that blonde dumb-bell. I'm sorry ... oh, dear, now we're both in the same boat. Miles is in love with you, I'm in love with Miles and you're in love with Guy ... what a mess!'

Karen could hardly believe it was true. 'So, you're in love with Miles?'

Mutely, Linda nodded, and fresh tears welled up in her eyes. 'You do see, I've got to go ...'

'No, I don't see at all,' said Karen, 'because Miles is not in love with me.'

Linda gaped. 'How do you know?'

'He told me. Miles is a lovely man, Linda, but only like a brother to me. I ... I think he might have been interested at first, because he was sorry for me, but as soon as you came up here ...'

Linda sighed. 'I hoped and hoped ... but when I arrived and saw you all starry-eyed, Miles attentive, I was sure I was too late.'

'You mean Miles was the real reason you wanted to come?' Karen was incredulous.

Linda drew her lips together. 'No, not altogether. I wanted you to find yourself again, Karen, and I would have come anyway, but with Miles here, there was an added incentive, shall we say.' She smiled weakly.

Karen laughed. 'I'm glad. I didn't want to be forever under an obligation to you. Linda, do you know what Miles thinks?'

'No, what?'

'That you're in love with Lou.'

'Lou Frinton! That's ridiculous!' She laughed ruefully. 'Oh, what a mess! I've been doing my best to keep away from Miles, determined you'd never find out how I felt, flirting madly with Lou and Guy and anyone else who happened along, and all for nothing.'

'I wonder,' said Karen, 'who Lou Frinton is in love with.'

Linda chuckled. 'Not with me! He's got a girl in Perth. She's going to join him up here as soon as she's done her social welfare course. She's hoping there'll be a job for her. They both like the outback.'

Karen relaxed. 'And Miles doesn't, not as a permanent way of life anyway, and you don't. You'd better start paying a little more attention to Miles, Linda.'

'He might not appreciate it.' Linda looked downcast again.

'I think he will,' said Karen firmly.

Linda glanced at her hopefully. 'Has he said ...'

Karen shook her head. 'There are some things, my girl, that you have to find out for yourself. But I'll say this. I don't think the cause is hopeless. A lot of people it seems have been hiding their true feelings around here.'

Linda's smile broadened as she hugged her knees. 'Gee ... if only ...' Then she looked with sympathy at her friend. 'But, Karen, what about you?'

'I'm leaving just as soon as I can,' Karen said. She was glad that there had been no need after all to explain about Guy's duplicity. That humiliation she could keep to herself. Linda must just believe that she was leaving for the same reason as she herself had been going to.

Now Linda would stay and Karen felt sure that she and Miles would come together. She hoped so. She loved them both and wanted them both for friends. They would come south again eventually, together, and she would meet up with them again when Guy was forgotten. She sighed deeply. Would she ever forget him?

That night she and Linda dined at the Club. Karen tried to put a brave face on it but she felt dreadfully depressed, and it was difficult to make cheerful conversation, as Linda was trying valiantly to do. After dinner they went into the lounge for coffee. Presently, they were joined by friends from the tennis club who introduced two strangers. One was Ivan Dailey, and the girl who introduced him to Karen said:

'You two will have something in common. Karen flies, too, Ivan. Ivan's on the last leg of a flight around Australia, Karen. He's a doctor.'

Karen smiled absently at the fair-haired young man who sat down next to her. Her thoughts were too far away to appreciate for a moment what a kindly hand in her affairs Fate had just taken.

'You must have had an interesting time,' she

remarked politely, and listened as he told her about the trip in the aircraft he had borrowed from a friend. His accent told her he was not Australian and in response to her queries he told her he was English, had recently qualified, and had decided to make this trip before he settled down to practice.

'Flying was always a hobby,' he said, 'and I wanted to do something adventurous, so I came out here in response to an invitation from a friend who owns the plane. I've had a fantastic time. In fact I'm thinking of trying to join the Flying Doctor Service. What do you think my chances are?'

It was then that the penny dropped and Karen knew that Fate had sent her Ivan Dailey.

'You could have my job if you wanted,' she said. 'I'm leaving.'

He looked surprised, and eager. 'Really? When?'

'As soon as someone can take over. But do you think you'd like it up here? It's pretty harsh at times, the climate I mean, the isolation, nothing like what you've been used to.'

'Which is why I'd love it,' he said simply. 'I'd already decided that this part of the world was for me. I didn't expect to find a chance ... are you sure?'

'I can't guarantee it,' she said carefully, 'but I feel sure Dr. Kendall will be anxious to take you on. He'll be back tomorrow or the next day, whenever the plane comes. Can you stick around to see him?'

'If there's a chance of a job in it, you bet I can!' said Ivan Dailey enthusiastically.

'You're staying at the hotel, I suppose?' When he nodded she said, 'I'll give you a call.'

'Thanks. I'll be waiting for it. Now, can I get you a drink? I feel the need to celebrate.'

Karen smiled. 'All right. It may be a bit premature, but I do feel sure that Guy will give you the job.'

As soon as Guy returned Karen made it her first task to see him and tell him her decision. She chose a time when she thought it unlikely they would be interrupted. She knocked briefly on his door.

'Come in!'

As she entered he looked up and when he saw it was she, he smiled and rose from his chair, coming round the desk towards her. The smile went straight to her heart and she desperately wanted to walk into those wide open arms, but common sense prevailed. It simply was not worth it, not even for one last passionate embrace, knowing how false it was and that he only meant to go on fooling her

269

until Saturday when Terri would announce their engagement.

Her look stopped him uncertainly and his arms fell to his sides.

'Karen, what's wrong? Darling ...?'

'I wish to speak to you,' she said tightly, moving away from him and sitting in the visitor's chair. 'I have something urgent to discuss.'

Her cold tone and frosty demeanour disconcerted him and, puzzled, he went back to his desk and sat down. 'Karen, what is this all about? You're staring at me as though I've got rabies or something. What's happened to you while I've been away? I thought we ... had begun to understand each other.'

She managed a short laugh. 'I'm sure you didn't take all that nonsense any more seriously than I did,' she said in a brittle tone. 'We had a bit of fun, Guy, but it wasn't meant to be serious, was it? I would have been going eventually once you found a replacement.'

'Karen, that's what I wanted to talk to you about ...'

'You've found someone?'

'No.'

'Good. Because I have.'

'*You* have!' His voice rose. 'What do you mean *you* have?'

'I've found someone to take my place. Just a lucky fluke really. I met this young English doctor at the Club. He's flown right round Australia in a Cessna and he can take over immediately, if you agree, of course. I'm sure you will when you meet him. He's just the man for the job, I'd say, young, single, well qualified, keen and sure to be reliable. I've offered to deliver his plane back to the friend in Perth he borrowed it from.'

'You mean you want to quit?' Guy said slowly. 'Right away?'

'Yes, I only agreed to stay until you found a replacement, didn't I?' she reminded him loftily. 'Well, I've found one for you. Ivan Dailey is his name. May I make an appointment for him to see you?' She added, 'I'd like to let him know as soon as possible, and I'd like to leave on Sunday.'

Guy's eyes narrowed. 'And I suppose I'll have Miles in here next, wanting to be let off his contract.' It was easy to see what was in his mind, what conclusion he had jumped to. Karen let him do it. He would find out soon enough that he was wrong, but meanwhile his revenge might not taste so sweet. He went on, 'So, you've had enough of Wirrumburra already?'

'As you said, it's a job for a man,' she said,

271

hating to give the impression she was giving, but that was better than having him believe he had humiliated her.

Her expression was derisive. 'So it was all talk at the start, all bluster, and you couldn't take it after all. I'm disappointed in you, Karen. I'd thought you were made of sterner stuff.'

She shrugged and rose. 'When shall I tell Dr. Dailey you'll see him?'

'This afternoon,' he said curtly. 'Four o'clock.'

'Very well. I'll let him know.' Karen walked out of the room without a backward glance. Guy did not try to prevent her. He did not catch her at the door and pull her into his arms as he had once done. Tears pricked her eyelids. It was all over.

Karen saw Ivan Dailey that afternoon as he was leaving after his interview with Guy. He was jubilant. Guy had accepted him for the job. Karen reaffirmed her offer to fly his Cessna back to Perth. She went home feeling numb.

Linda was glum when she told her the outcome. 'I'll miss you, Karen. When are you leaving?'

'I told him I wanted to go on Sunday. He didn't object.'

'I don't suppose you'll be going to Terri's party,' Linda said gloomily.

'Hardly. I'm not on shift but I'll volunteer to swap with someone.'

'I will, too,' said Linda. 'I don't think I could bear it, either. It seems odd her even asking us nurses anyway. I thought she despised us. I wonder why she did.'

Karen knew why now. It would have been Guy's idea to ensure that her humiliation was complete and he there to witness it. If she hadn't been rostered as off duty he would no doubt have found a way to arrange it so that she could go to the party. And if she hadn't overheard that conversation she would have gone, all unsuspecting. Well, at least she wouldn't be giving him the satisfaction of his revenge now. She had turned the tables on him by resigning and pretending it had all been a joke. He did not know that she knew the truth. The engagement was a well-kept secret, so he must believe what she had said. He might even be feeling a little humiliated himself—she certainly hoped so. She ought to be laughing at that but she wasn't. She just wanted to cry.

Late on Saturday afternoon Karen was at home at Ma Carson's doing some ironing, as it was not yet time for her to go on duty, when the telephone rang. A moment later Ma Carson burst into the room where Karen was at work.

'Karen, it's an emergency!'

'Oh, no!' Karen switched off the iron, replaced it on the stand and ran to the phone.

Guy barked at her. 'A young child is seriously ill. I'll pick you up in five minutes.'

Karen's breath caught in her throat. An emergency at this eleventh hour! And tomorrow she would be gone and never have to go on one with Guy again. She didn't want to go now. She had a sudden inspiration.

'Why don't you get Dr. Dailey to take you?' she said. 'It would be good experience for him.'

Instantly Guy's voice crackled savagely back down the line, 'May I remind you, Sister Lalor, that Dr. Dailey does not commence his duties until Monday? You are still in my employ. Be ready in five minutes!'

She wanted to refuse point blank but she could not. She was still in his employ and while she argued a child might die. She steeled herself and went with him.

It was a tense flight. Few words passed between them. Guy was clearly chagrined because she had outwitted him by resigning and finding her own replacement. As he couldn't humiliate her or punish her any other way, he was determined to make her do her duty until the last possible minute.

It was a bit of an anti-climax when the emergency proved to be a false alarm. The boy had nothing more than a high temperature resulting from a bout of flu that had been going around recently, and over-anxious parents who had panicked. Guy decided there was no need to take the child in to hospital.

'Parents tend to worry more when help isn't close at hand,' he said as they became airborne again. 'You can hardly blame them. Kids are always giving them frights, and that family hasn't been living up here for long. The child will respond to the antibiotics and be fit as a fiddle in a few days.'

Karen said nothing. She was acutely aware that this was the last flight she would make with Guy. She was so preoccupied with her thoughts that she did not notice the swirling dust below until they were almost above it. Before she could take evasive action they were suddenly caught in a fierce wind current and hurled upwards as though some giant hand had plucked them off their course.

'Hell, a cockeyed bob!' exclaimed Guy. 'Get out of it, quick!'

That was easier said than done. Struggling

275

with the controls, Karen's first instinct was to go higher, but even as she attempted it, the plane's single engine stalled. The silence was deafening. Guy shot a startled look at her. She could not have spoken to reassure him if she had wanted to. It was all she could manage to battle with the swirling redness around them and try to start the engine again. To her relief it fired but spluttered ominously, and the little plane bucked and rocked in an alarming fashion, far worse than on the day she had made Guy sick.

Now there was no way she could go higher to escape the whirling desert storm. They were losing height rapidly and the dust was growing thicker. She could see nothing. It was far worse than flying at night.

One thought kept hammering her brain. Why hadn't she seen the dust storm? Why hadn't Guy?

For the first time fear rose in her throat. She was in a situation where she didn't know what to do. All she knew was that she was going to have to make an emergency landing—and soon. She must set the plane down while she still had some power, or they were finished. She battled for what seemed an eternity with unco-operative controls, trying to keep the machine from diving into a spin. Her arms felt as though they were being wrenched from the sockets, until suddenly, without warning, the buffeting stopped, the dust was no longer swirling but falling like red rain past the cockpit windows. There was time to make a brief distress call on the radio and yell to Guy, 'For God's sake fasten your seat belt!' as she saw the ground coming up much too fast to meet them.

Now she saw that there was nothing below but hummocky hills and patches of spinifex, clumps of straggly trees. There was nowhere she could land with a good chance of survival. Then, miraculously, as they skimmed a low rise she saw the creek bed, almost straight ahead, flat, smooth, like a runway. She prayed that what looked like a smooth sandy floor was not just a thin covering over jagged rocks. She had no choice but to chance it.

The engine finally puttered out when they were only a few metres above the ground. Karen held on with all her might and fought to keep the plane between the creek banks. Suddenly red dust swirled over them and the *Jabiru* ditched with a tremendous jolt and a sound of rippling metal. Karen had only had time to think that it was the final irony that she should die out here, with Guy, and then everything went black.

CHAPTER THIRTEEN

Karen woke to a stinging pain in her shoulder and cried out.

'Sorry!' It was Guy's voice, distant, as though lost in a fog.

Karen moved and a sharp jab knifed her shoulder again. It jerked her into full consciousness and she remembered what had happened. Her eyes lighted first on the plane, glinting in the sunlight, fifty metres away, its tail at an unnatural angle. All she could think of were Guy's words many weeks ago, 'Have you had any experience of cock-eyed bobs?' She had been so confident then that she could cope with anything.

'You're all right,' said Guy reassuring now. 'The radio's okay and I've spoken to Base and told them what's happened.'

She became aware of her surroundings as he was speaking. She was lying on her side beneath a scrubby tree in the shade, and as she turned her head she saw Guy's fingers cleansing a gash in her shoulder. He had ripped out her sleeve and she saw that the front of her shirt was torn and unbuttoned. He had unhooked the bra strap from the cup to bare her shoulder and momentarily she recalled that night at Wirrumburra Downs when she had lain beside him on the cane lounger and he had caressed her. She closed her eyes again just as he turned to look at her.

'I'm afraid it will hurt a bit,' Guy said. 'It's not bleeding much, it's just a flesh wound luckily, but I'll put a couple of stitches in it. I don't think it will leave a scar.'

He went on dabbing at the wound, holding a small kidney dish under her armpit. She noticed the medical kit open beside him.

'Are you all right?' she asked quaveringly.

'Yes, a couple of scratches, that's all. I don't think you've broken anything. I carried you as far away from the fuselage as possible in case it decided to blow up.'

Karen's eyes met his. 'I should have seen that dust storm and avoided it,' she said, agonised by the knowledge of her incompetency.

There was no censure in his gaze, however. 'So should I,' he said firmly. 'But I'm afraid we were both too preoccupied.'

She looked away. 'You should have let Dr. Dailey fly you,' she said bitterly.

He placed a pad of lint on her shoulder and bandaged it, not speaking until it was finished.

Then he said, 'How does it feel?'

'Much better, thanks.'

'Take these.' He offered her two aspirins and handed her a mug of water from the emergency can they always carried. Then he chuckled. 'I'm afraid you're going to have a beautiful shiner tomorrow!'

She had been vaguely aware of impaired sight. Now she raised tentative fingers to touch her left eye. It felt tender and puffy.

'I must have hit my head as we crashed.'

'We didn't crash, we landed,' he corrected emphatically.

'Poor *Jabiru*. Alex will never forgive me.'

Guy glanced towards the aircraft. 'I don't think there's a great deal of damage to it. A side panel was ripped off and I suspect the wheels are in a mess, judging by the way she's ended up. But you can go down there and see for yourself as soon as you feel well enough. How you managed to land it at all is a miracle. Some pilot, you!'

She could not help feeling cheered by his compliment and yet it did not entirely dissipate the shame she felt for not having seen the danger and avoided it. She struggled to her feet, but stumbled, so that he was obliged to catch her to steady her, one hand on her un-injured shoulder, one around her waist. He pressed her against him and whispered huskily, 'Karen ... thank God you're all right.'

For a moment she almost laid her head thankfully against his chest and said how relieved she was that he was not dead, and then she realised that things were not as she wanted them to be. She pulled away, stepping back abruptly from him.

'Guy, really ... how could you ... now ...'

He moved towards her. 'Karen, now is the time I've most wanted to hold you in my arms, to ...'

'You're despicable!' she spat at him, and stumbled down to where the plane lay.

He ran after her and caught up with her, snatching at her hand and pulling her round to face him. She winced at the pain in her shoulder but he was not concerned about that now.

'Despicable! That's a very strong word. What have I done to deserve it? I would have thought it applied more precisely to you!'

'Me!'

'Yes, you made me believe you loved me, but all the time you were simply making a fool out of me.'

She laughed without mirth. 'One revenge

deserves another.'

'Revenge? Now what are you talking about?'

'I knew what you were up to, Guy, don't worry. I'm not as green as you imagined. I know a conceited, arrogant man when I see one. You couldn't bear me to have the last word, could you?'

'I think that blow on the head has deranged you,' he said. 'You'd better come back and sit down quietly in the shade until you feel better.'

'I'm not the one who's deranged,' she retorted. 'Anyone who would do what you did would have to be, though. To think that even now, on the day of your engagement party ...' She suddenly began to laugh. 'Oh, that's amusing, that really is! Everybody there at the Club and the most important guest, bar one of course, won't be present!' She giggled hysterically.

Guy released her hand and ceased trying to pull her back up the slope. He simply bent his large frame and scooped her up in his arms and carried her, struggling, back to the shade of the tree.

'Don't struggle,' he rapped angrily. 'You'll burst those stitches.'

'Put me down!'

He sat her on the blanket which he had spread out for her to lie on before. When she

282

tried to get up he pinned her ankles with an iron grip.

'For heaven's sake, Karen, do you want me to slap your face, too?'

Her hysteria subsided only fractionally. 'That's what I ought to do to you!' She raised her hand and held it back ready to strike him. As her palm shot forward he grabbed it and with his other hand slapped her cheek, not hard, but enough to shock her. She started crying. He let go and said quietly:

'You're suffering from shock. I don't think you know what you are saying.'

She lifted her tear-stained face, not caring any more, not even wanting to run away, wishing she had died after all.

'You won't be able to go to the party,' she said, chokingly, 'We'll never get out of here in time ... I've ruined that, too ...' She felt all churned up inside. He was right. She didn't know what she was saying. Why should she care if he didn't make it to his own engagement party?

He was looking at her with a puzzled expression. 'Party? You mean Terri's birthday party, I suppose. Well, there's no need to fret about that. I wasn't going and neither were you according to the roster.' He seemed genuinely unable to understand her concern.

Karen was equally perplexed. 'But Terri wouldn't announce it without you being there.'

'What?' His eyes had narrowed suspiciously.

'Her engagement, of course!'

'How do you know about that? It was supposed to be a secret.'

Karen felt the ground slipping away from her, but she was not sure why.

'I overheard her telling some friends that she was going to Perth to choose the ring, and that she was going to announce her engagement to you at her birthday party.'

'To me!' His eyebrows had shot up. 'She said that?'

'Well, she didn't actually say *you,* but ... well, you're always together and everyone thought ...' She trailed away, aware that she must have made a ghastly mistake and yet unable to believe that there could have been any doubt.

Guy's face was grim. 'Other people always know one's business better than oneself,' he observed bitterly. 'Especially in small communities. I have never had the slightest intention of marrying Terri Lawson. Good heavens, Karen, surely you couldn't see her as my wife!'

'Well ...' She shrugged. 'What else was I to think?'

'I thought I had made it very clear that the

woman I married would have to be very special indeed. Terri Lawson is not that kind of woman.'

'I know.' Karen felt utterly deflated. 'I made a mistake. I'm sorry. Maybe you're not quite as despicable as I thought, but you can't deny you deliberately set out to take revenge for what I did.'

'Ah ... now we're coming to it, the bit I don't understand at all. For what would I seek revenge and how, may I ask, am I supposed to have been doing it?'

He was bluffing, she was sure. She said, 'You were livid that day I hurled you round the sky and made you airsick. Miles said I'd better watch out because you weren't the kind to take that sort of treatment lightly from a woman. I couldn't imagine what you might do until ...'

'Until what ...?'

'Until ... you made a pass at me in the pantry that night!'

He chuckled softly at the memory. 'A pass! That's a nice old-fashioned phrase. But I can't see how it could be called revenge.'

'Oh, you're so arrogant,' she burst out, 'you were so damned sure you could make me fall in love with you ...'

'Yes, after that night I did think it might

285

not be impossible.'

He looked so smug about it that she flared anew. 'Well, it was impossible! It was all pretence on my part. I was wise to you, Guy Kendall. I knew what you were up to so I played you at your own game. I just let you think you'd won.'

'So that's what it was all about,' he murmured, smiling infuriatingly at her. 'Now I see. That's why you resigned. Yes, I see it all now, but just in case, why don't you spell it all out in detail for me, there's a good girl, so I can set you straight on a few things.'

She didn't want to. She closed her lips firmly and refused to say another word. She would not let him humiliate her any more. She wanted to run but there was nowhere to run to. She could only turn her head away from him.

He moved to sit beside her. He did not touch her. He simply said, 'Karen, please believe that I never once had any thought of revenge. I swear it. Now tell me everything.'

In spite of her resolve she told him. It was a relief in a way to let it all spill out. As she finally ran out of words he slid his hand over hers.

'So you weren't playing along, pretending, when you said you loved me, you meant it?'

'I'm afraid so.' She hung her head despairingly. It didn't even matter now.

'Karen,' he said, 'now I'm going to tell you a few things ... things I wanted to tell you that night at home on the verandah ... the night we were called to an emergency before I could ...' He paused briefly and linked his fingers with hers and she did not try to pull her hand away. He went on, 'Believe me, if you can, that the first moment I set eyes on you, something extraordinary happened to me ...'

'But you tried to send me away!' she exclaimed, facing him now, wide-eyed.

'I know. There was a reason for that reaction. I was afraid of what might happen if I let you stay. I knew I was going to be vulnerable and I didn't want to be.'

'Because of your mother ... and Mary ...' murmured Karen.

'Yes,' he said simply, not asking how she knew. 'I had lost the two women I had loved most—I had lost my father as well—I suppose I thought I was jinxed, and I couldn't bear to lose anyone else. I was afraid to fall in love for that reason.'

'But in the end you did let me stay,' she said.

He laughed softly. 'Because in the end, love proved to be a much stronger emotion than fear.'

'So soon?' She was stunned.

'So soon. At least I didn't call it love to myself, all I knew was that I couldn't let you go. I wanted you to fall in love with me and at first I thought it was a hopeless cause because you hated me so much and anyway there was Miles ... but the first time I kissed you told me I had a chance.'

'But, Guy,' Karen objected, 'you've just said again that the girl you marry must be someone special. I'm not ...'

He placed a finger across her lips. 'Karen, my dear love, do you know what I mean by special? My special woman is a woman who can stand on her own two feet, who has the courage of her convictions and will defy any man who tries to put her down. She isn't even afraid to make a fool of him when he deserves it.

'She's a woman who can do the circuits with me without fuss, efficiently, and refuses to admit when she's dead on her feet. She's a woman who can put me down gently in a creek bed, get hurt herself, and worry because I'm late for my engagement party ...' He spoke the last words mockingly, laughing softly as he drew her gently into his arms. 'Karen, my special woman has long shapely legs, a flat belly, smooth round breasts that fit snugly into

288

my palms. She has hair the colour of sunset and eyes like the still waters of the gorge, and a mouth so sweet and tender ...'

His lips touched hers and all the fires she had so valiantly tried to extinguish leapt into fresh life immediately.

'... and her name is Karen Lalor.'

The kiss lingered and when he withdrew his lips from hers she said, 'But if you're not getting engaged to Terri, who is?'

'Ruben Arnstein! Remember, the hunting, shooting, fishing tycoon from Texas? She told me about it on the plane going down to Perth, quite apologetically! He met her at the airport.'

Karen sighed. What a crazy mess it had all been. How hopelessly mistaken she had been about everything.

'Guy,' she ventured a few moments later, 'how long will it take for help to reach us?'

Guy glanced at the sky. The sun had almost gone and a pale rosy haze was tinting the sky and the rugged red hills were slowly turning purple. A cool breeze stirred the scrubby trees. It would soon be night.

'They won't set out until daylight. I told them we had emergency rations and water on the plane and neither of us was badly hurt.' He looked down lovingly at her. 'I, for one, won't mind if they don't hurry. We've still got quite a lot more to say to each other, I think.'

Karen smiled happily at him. 'It will make a nice change to be quite alone without the danger of anyone interrupting.' A thought suddenly occurred to her and made her chuckle inwardly. 'Guy, you weren't airsick this time in spite of the buffeting we had!'

He laughed. 'No! And I've never been airsick in my life before that other time. Must have been something we had for lunch!'

As they were laughing about it, an interruption came. The sound of aircraft engines shattered the stillness and a few moments later a light plane passed over their heads. Guy immediately leapt up and ran down to their plane, waving. At first Karen thought they had not been seen but then she saw the aircraft turn, circle and come back. It circled very low over them and she waved, too, to show she was all right.

As the plane came in very low, she recognised the pilot. 'It's Ivan Dailey!' she exclaimed. The pilot grinned and waved and the next moment there was a small parachute floating down to earth, a metal canister attached to it. Guy retrieved it as the plane roared off into the distance.

'What is it?' Karen joined him as he was opening it.

Guy was chuckling. He drew out a corrugated cardboard-wrapped parcel and ripped it open. He held up a bottle of champagne.

'And not a drop spilled!' he exclaimed triumphantly.

Karen was astonished. She groped for the note she had seen fall from the parcel. She read it and then looked at Guy accusingly.

'What does it say?' he asked.

'Congratulations on your engagement. Happy landings',' she read out. ' "Love from Linda and all at Wirrumburra Hospital".' She swallowed hard as she faced him. 'Guy ... what did you say to them?'

'I said I thought we ought to have something to go with the tinned sausages and peas in case we had something to celebrate. Linda evidently thought champagne would be fitting!'

'You were jumping to conclusions, weren't you?'

He was unrepentant. 'No. You see I spoke to Linda on the radio and she had apparently just found out that Terri was getting engaged to Arnstein, not me. She was, bless her, very blunt about how she saw things between you and me.'

'But she didn't know that you ...'

'No, but she reckoned it was worth telling me how you really felt about me.'

Karen hung her head. 'And you let me rave at you ...'

He cradled her head against him. 'You're so lovely when you're afire like that! I should have known that shock might make you hysterical, though. I'm sorry, love.'

She clung to him thankfully. After a moment she said hesitantly, 'Guy ... you'll still let me fly?'

He tightened his arms around her. 'What chance would I have if I tried to stop you? I wouldn't want the wrath of your Irish ancestors down on my head a second time. You will, I'm afraid, always do what you want to do, my love, and with my blessing. But I'll keep an eye on you. Overdo it and you'll be grounded. I'm still boss at the hospital, remember.' He tilted her chin and looked deeply into her eyes. 'There's just one thing I'm going to insist on and you've got to say yes to that right now.'

'What's that?'

'That you'll marry me! You haven't said yes, yet.'

'You've only just asked me!' Karen slid her arms around his neck and looked into his dear face and murmured, 'Yes, Guy, of course I'll marry you.'

Night came down like an enveloping cloak

and as the fire burned low and the stars came out, Guy wrapped Karen in a blanket with another rolled up to support her head and injured shoulder. Feeling a little tipsy from the champagne which they had drunk from plastic beakers, Karen snuggled down contentedly beside Guy, sleeping almost at once.

She woke later with a start when an owl called eerily and a dingo barked distantly. Guy was sitting up with a blanket around his shoulders, wide awake, staring into the night. Karen reached out her hand and he clasped it.

'It's all right, my sweet, I'm here,' he whispered.

Karen closed her eyes again. It would always be all right, she thought, so long as Guy was there to love and protect her, every night of her life.